PRAISE FOR *THE SEC*

"Like a younger version of Ann Brashares's *The Sisterhood of the Traveling Pants*, this book details how the girls bake and send each other cookies at what turn out to be critical times in the school year. . . . The variety of families depicted is refreshing. . . . Recipes are included. . . . Readers will enjoy getting to know the campers from Flowerpot Cabin and baking—and tasting—the included cookie recipes."

—*School Library Journal*

"The smooth writing and quick pacing make the pages fly by, as does Freeman's clever technique of leaving each girl's story unfinished until her letter to the next girl clears up loose ends. . . . Hand this to the BFFs who aren't quite ready for Brashares's *The Sisterhood of the Traveling Pants*."

—*The Bulletin*

Also by Martha Freeman

CAMPFIRE COOKIES

MARTHA FREEMAN

THE SECRET COOKIE CLUB

A Paula Wiseman Book

Simon & Schuster Books
for Young Readers

New York   London
Toronto   Sydney   New Delhi

SIMON & SCHUSTER BOOKS FOR YOUNG READERS

An imprint of Simon & Schuster Children's Publishing Division

1230 Avenue of the Americas, New York, New York 10020

This book is a work of fiction. Any references to historical events, real people, or real places are used fictitiously. Other names, characters, places, and events are products of the author's imagination, and any resemblance to actual events or places or persons, living or dead, is entirely coincidental.

Text copyright © 2015 by Martha Freeman

Jacket and chapter opener illustrations copyright © 2015 by Brenna Vaughn

All rights reserved, including the right of reproduction in whole or in part in any form.

SIMON & SCHUSTER BOOKS FOR YOUNG READERS is a trademark of Simon & Schuster, Inc.

For information about special discounts for bulk purchases, please contact Simon & Schuster Special Sales at 1-866-506-1949 or business@simonandschuster.com.

The Simon & Schuster Speakers Bureau can bring authors to your live event. For more information or to book an event, contact the Simon & Schuster Speakers Bureau at 1-866-248-3049 or visit our website at www.simonspeakers.com.

Also available in a Simon & Schuster Books for Young Readers hardcover edition

Book design by Krista Vossen

The text for this book was set in Kepler Std.

Manufactured in the United States of America

1118 OFF

First Simon & Schuster Books for Young Readers paperback edition May 2016

4 6 8 10 9 7 5

The Library of Congress has cataloged the hardcover edition as follows:

Freeman, Martha, 1956-

The Secret Cookie Club / Martha Freeman.

pages cm

"A Paula Wiseman Book."

Summary: Four very different girls meet at Moonlight Ranch camp and decide to remain friends all year by exchanging letters and homemade cookies, using recipes their counselor's grandfather passed along.

ISBN 978-1-4814-1046-5 (hardcover)—ISBN 978-1-4814-1047-2 (pbk)—ISBN 978-1-4814-1048-9 (ebook)

[1. Friendship—Fiction. 2. Schools—Fiction. 3. Family life—Fiction. 4. Cookies—Fiction. 5. Clubs—Fiction.] I. Title.

PZ7.F87496Sec 2015

[Fic]—dc23

2014025949

For the Schoenholtz family: David, Jack, Marya, Hannah, Isaac,
Saul, Joseph, and Millie
—M. A. F.

CHAPTER 1

Monday, July 6, Moonlight Ranch

Hannah lay on her top bunk listening to rain and staring at gloom. She was worried. Tomorrow was Grace's tenth birthday, and not one of the three other campers in Flowerpot Cabin cared.

In the distance, thunder rumbled, and then the rain let up. Hannah was from New York City. The summer camp was in Arizona. It was Hannah's first year as a counselor there, and after a week, she was getting used to these brief nighttime storms. Now she rolled over, closed her eyes, and tried her usual strategy for falling asleep—counting backward from one hundred. By eighty-six, she was worrying again: The real problem wasn't Grace. It was all of them.

The four girls in Flowerpot Cabin simply didn't like each other.

Take that morning during chores. It had been Emma's turn to do inspection. When Emma pointed out the streaks Olivia left on the bathroom mirror, Olivia handed Emma the rag. "If you don't like it, you do it!"

Hearing this, Grace had said, "Too early for yelling," and walked out.

As for Lucy—she wasn't paying attention. While Emma and Olivia were quarreling, she had stood precariously on a chair, using a drinking glass to rescue a spider from the ceiling.

Remembering this, Hannah sighed and pulled up her covers.

The trouble was the four girls were very different—different backgrounds, different interests, different temperaments.

Olivia was the drama queen—in both the best sense and the worst. She was tall and lovely and graceful with real singing and acting talent. For her, everything that happened was either *really, really* awesome or *really, really* dumb. She had enough chutzpah—as Hannah's parents would say—to fill the horse barn twice over.

Emma was organized, a worrier, and—to be honest—a bit of a klutz. She had fallen off her horse twice the first week, but both times she'd bounced up again, insisting she was fine. To get out of square dancing, she'd volunteered to pick up litter. The other girls thought Emma was bossy, but Hannah didn't agree. Emma was more like a mother hen, concerned for the well-being of everyone she knew. For the pool, she packed extra sunscreen.

Grace was different—tidy, precise, and good at every-thing she tried, especially music. She was also quiet and serious. At the same time, she had a secret—a funny one. She kept a private, personal stash of Oreos hidden under a washcloth in her bathroom cubby. Hannah had found them by accident one morning when she reached into Grace's cubby instead of her own. Because food might attract bugs or field mice, campers were supposed to keep it in closed metal containers. To prevent bad feelings, campers were also supposed to share any treats they had. This meant perfect, obedient Grace was breaking two rules with her hidden Oreo cookies!

Maybe, Hannah thought, Grace needs to have her own little secret if she is going to stay otherwise perfect and obedient. In any case, Hannah would never tell.

The last camper in Flowerpot Cabin was Lucy, who was blond and carelessly pretty. She liked to paint and draw. She didn't seem to notice or care what anyone else thought of her. Lost in her own thoughts most of the time, she had been half an hour late to dinner the second evening because she couldn't find the dining hall. Unlike the other girls—unlike pretty much anyone else at Moonlight Ranch—she came from a family without much money, a family she never talked about.

Hannah rolled over again and sighed. Maybe it was all her fault. She was the counselor. She should do something to promote peace, love, and understanding. But what?

Still worrying, Hannah drifted off to sleep and

dreamed. It was almost morning when her grandfather made an appearance. He had been dead for five years— since Hannah was fourteen—and she was glad to see him. That night he was mixing cookie dough in the kitchen of the delicatessen in Manhattan where he had worked. His cheeks were flushed from the oven's heat. He was smiling.

"Hannahla, try this." He offered an oatmeal raisin cookie. "You know what I always say about flour power."

This was an old joke between them, and Hannah knew she was supposed to spell it out: "F-L-O-U-R!"

After that, the camp bell rang—time to wake up. Hannah opened her eyes, thinking she could still smell the cinnamon. *It's a shame I didn't get to eat the cookie*, she thought.

But her mood was lighter. She had an idea.

The Moonlight Ranch Summer Camp is located an hour north of Phoenix in the Arizona desert. Arrayed in a stand of cottonwood trees, it consists of forty cabins behind split-rail fences on either side of a dirt road—girls' cabins to the right, boys' to the left. The dining hall and kitchen are near the entrance gate, a wooden arch topped by a metal sculpture of a full moon with a laughing face. The pond, horse barn, playing fields, show ring, and outbuildings are over a hill where the road dead-ends. Beyond that, cattle graze.

After the campfire that evening, Hannah led the four girls of Flowerpot Cabin up the road toward the camp kitchen.

Grace walked beside her. "Aren't we going to get in trouble?" she asked. "It's almost lights-out."

"We have special permission," Hannah said.

"Is this something to do with Grace's birthday?" Emma asked.

"Ma-a-aybe," Hannah said.

"That means yes," Olivia said, "in grown-up talk."

"Who are you calling a grown-up?" asked Hannah.

"You don't have to notice my birthday," Grace said. "I don't mind."

Lucy said, "What birthday?"

As they neared the kitchen, Hannah was surprised to see lights on. Inside, she was even more surprised to see a boy. She knew he was from Lasso Cabin, which made him aged ten to eleven, but she couldn't remember his name.

"I'm allowed," he said instead of hello. "I asked the cook."

"Well, I asked her too," said Hannah. "What are you making?"

"Cupcakes." The boy pointed at a mixing bowl full of batter. "I'm Vivek."

"Where's your counselor?" Hannah asked.

"Getting the other guys to shut up," Vivek said. "I'm the only good one in my cabin. Not to brag or anything."

Emma nodded. "Everybody knows about Lasso Cabin."

"OMG, are we making *cupcakes*?" Olivia asked. "How totally fabulous!"

"I like cupcakes," Lucy said, "with white frosting and sprinkles."

"We are making cookies," said Hannah. "Because my grandpa was a baker, and he believed in flour power. Get it?"

"You mean like f-l-o-u-r?" Grace asked.

"I don't get it," said Lucy.

"You'll see," said Hannah.

"Why is Vivek making cupcakes?" Grace asked.

"Hello?" said Vivek. "I'm right here, and it's not like I can't hear you. I'm making cupcakes to mail to my mom for her birthday."

"Wait—so that's whose birthday?" said Lucy.

"Cupcakes are really, *really* a lot of work," said Olivia. "You should buy her earrings."

"I don't have any money," Vivek said.

"You don't?" Olivia said.

"Not everyone has money," said Emma.

"Okay, ladies." Hannah pulled a recipe card from her pocket. "Lucy—you've been poking around. Can you find measuring spoons and cups, a rubber scraper, and two bowls? Grace, you get the eggs and the butter from the refrigerator. Vivek, are you done with that mixer?"

While Hannah read the directions aloud, the girls measured, sifted, creamed, and combined—eating only small bits of soft, sweet dough and making only a moderate mess. Then they rolled out the cookies, cut them, and placed them one by one on cookie sheets.

They had just begun to sprinkle sugar when Emma

frowned and said, "Does anybody else smell smoke?"

"My cupcakes!" Vivek moved to open the oven. Emma handed him oven mitts. Inside, instead of cupcakes, there were twelve black and shrunken cinders, which immediately set off the smoke detector. Hannah hurried to open a window, and a gust of wind blew in, silencing the squawk and announcing the evening thunderstorm.

Vivek was crushed. "I must've set the oven too high. Now what am I supposed to do?"

For a second, it was quiet.

Then Lucy said, "If you frost them enough, maybe your mom won't notice."

And Olivia laughed. "That is the *dumbest* idea I ever heard."

Lucy looked at her toes. "My mom wouldn't notice."

"Send her some of Grace's cookies," said Emma.

"Naturally, Emma has the answer," said Olivia.

"Have you got a better one?" asked Emma.

"I don't mind sharing," said Grace.

"It's a better idea than mine," said Lucy.

Emma looked at Olivia. "What do you think, O?

Give some of our cookies to Vivek's mom or not?"

"O?" Olivia looked at Emma. "Is that supposed to be me now?"

Emma shrugged. "If you want."

Olivia sighed theatrically. "I am *entirely* certain that Vivek's mom would prefer earrings. At the same time, I am not one to be selfish. "Also,"—she looked shy all of a sudden—"if you guys want to call me 'O,' that would be cool."

Hannah couldn't believe it. *Kind of, sort of . . .* the girls of Flowerpot Cabin might be beginning to get along.

A few minutes later, the sugar cookies came out of the oven, and they were perfect. Placed on wire racks, they cooled quickly. Then Grace helped Vivek pack a dozen into a tin for his mom while Olivia, Lucy, and Emma cleaned up, and Hannah poured glasses of milk.

Outside, rain fell and thunder rumbled, then a flash of lightning and—*crack*—the lights in the kitchen went black.

Everybody squealed. Then everybody started talking at once: "Don't panic!" "Find a flashlight!" "Who's panicking?" "I found birthday candles." "Somebody stepped on my toe!" "Sorry." "Sorry." *"Ouch!"* "Sorry."

It took a few minutes, but finally all five girls and one boy were gathered around a plate of cookies, ten of them stuck with birthday candles. In the dark, the tiny flames cast a warm and cheerful glow.

Lucy said, "I thought it was Vivek's mom's birthday."

Grace said, "It's *my* birthday."

Lucy said, "What a coincidence! Happy birthday!"

After that, everybody sang, and Grace blew out her candles.

From that night on, every girl in Flowerpot Cabin loved every other girl in Flowerpot Cabin every moment all summer long.

Not.

But Emma, Olivia, Grace, and Lucy did have a special flour-power bond, which paid off when they won the cabin competition for cleanest bathroom, got second place at the talent show and the girls' prize in the egg-and-spoon relay on Game Day.

CHAPTER 2

Thursday, August 11

The night before the last day of camp, the girls of Flowerpot Cabin were in their bunks. There was a lot for the counselors to do at the close of the season, and Hannah had been up since six that morning. She was exhausted, but she couldn't help overhearing her campers' whispered conversation.

"What if we all go home and forget each other?" Emma said. "What if we don't stay friends?"

"That would be really, really, really *sad*!" said Olivia.

"Three *really*s," said Lucy.

"When is it we first started to like each other?" Emma asked.

"Oh, Emma. Not another quiz. I am *too* sleepy," said Olivia.

Grace spoke up. "It was on my birthday—when we made the cookies with Vivek."

"With *Vive-e-ek*," Olivia teased.

"Leave her alone, O," said Emma. "She can't help it that she thinks he's cute."

"Is he cute?" asked Lucy.

"According to some people," said Olivia.

"Listen, do you want to hear my idea or not?" said Emma. "Here it is: What if all year long we send each other cookies?"

"Okay," said Lucy. "And I'll go first because otherwise I'll forget."

"Hello-o-o?" said Olivia. "We didn't even agree to do it yet."

"When school starts—and piano and dance—I'm

going to be really busy," said Grace.

"That's what I'm worried about," said Emma. "Even though we're all superbusy, we have to take time out to stay friends. We have to make a commitment."

"I won't be that busy," said Lucy.

"Lucky," said Grace.

"What kind of cookies?" Lucy asked.

"Sugar," said Olivia. "I mean, *if* it's happening, they should be sugar."

"Doesn't have to be," said Emma. "It can be whatever kind you think goes with whoever's getting the cookies."

"Oh, I get it," said Grace. "So, like, if I have a piano recital coming up, and it's Emma's turn to send cookies, then Emma sends me the best kind of cookies for practicing piano."

"Or if my mom has another new boyfriend, I get the best kind of cookie to survive a mom romance," said Lucy.

"Or if my brother's baseball team loses the state championship, I get cookies for when my whole family is in mourning except I don't actually even care," said Olivia.

"Exactly," said Emma.

"We need a name," said Olivia.

"I'm bad at naming things," Lucy said. "How about the Cookie Society?"

"The *Secret* Cookie Society," said Grace, "because we're not going to tell anybody. It's just us."

"My aunt Freda's in a society," said Lucy. "They do projects to help people."

"We don't have to help people, do we?" Olivia asked.

"We helped Vivek when we shared our cookies," said Grace.

"He can't be in the club. He's not in Flowerpot Cabin," said Emma.

"Also, he's a boy," said Olivia.

"I noticed that too," said Lucy.

"We could send him cookies, though, couldn't we?" said Grace. "Like, without telling him who they're from. Like a prank, only a nice prank."

"Grace, do you have a crush on Vivek?" Emma asked.

"*No!*" said Grace.

"That means you do," said Olivia.

"It should be 'club' instead of 'society,'" said Lucy. "'Club' is easier to spell."

"Time to vote," said Emma. "All in favor of Secret Cookie Club, say 'aye'!"

"Aye!" said everybody.

After that, they figured out the schedule. Lucy would send the first batch of cookies to Grace in the fall. Grace would send cookies to Emma around New Year's. Emma would send cookies to Olivia in the winter, and Olivia would send cookies to Lucy in the spring.

"How will we know what kind of cookie to send?" Olivia wanted to know.

"That's the whole point," said Emma. "The only way we know is if we stay in touch."

"And Vivek?" Grace said.

But Hannah didn't hear the answer. She had fallen asleep, smiling. She was dreaming of flour power.

CHAPTER 3

Saturday, August 13, Grace

"Grace, sweetie, are you okay? It's getting late!" Hannah, our counselor, called through the bathroom door, which, unfortunately, did not have a lock. If Hannah or anyone found out I had just vomited my breakfast, I would die of embarrassment.

"Yes. Fine. Don't come in." I flushed the toilet, rinsed my mouth out, splashed water on my face, and looked around for my towel before remembering it was packed in my trunk, just like everything else.

"Grace?" Hannah sounded worried.

I opened the door. My face was dripping.

"Hold on. I think I saw paper towels." Hannah found a crumpled-looking roll in Flowerpot Cabin's mostly empty cupboards and handed it over. "Now tell me what's the matter."

Usually I appreciated Hannah's TLC. We all did. But right then I wanted to be left alone.

"I am *fine*," I said, then realized how that sounded and added, "Sorry." I took a final swipe at my face, wadded the towel, and threw it away.

Would we lose points for the wastebasket not being empty?

Oh, right. The Chore Score didn't matter now. Camp was over. Today we were going home.

"I'm just upset about saying good-bye," I said.

This was true, but it wasn't everything. A few kids had already been bused to the airport in Phoenix, but most people's parents were coming by car this morning to pick them up. That included the parents of us four campers in Flowerpot Cabin—Emma, Olivia, Lucy, and me.

More than anything else, I was freaking out—as Lucy would say—about my parents meeting everyone else's. My parents aren't like other people's. My parents have accents. My parents dress too nicely. My parents are ten to the tenth power more embarrassing than anyone else's parents in the entire United States of America.

The worried knot in my stomach persisted even though now the pancakes were out of the way.

Hannah stepped back, looked at me, and shrugged. "Okay, Grace, my friend, if you say so." Then she steered me toward the door with a hand on my shoulder. "Everybody else is on the oval waiting for their parents already. I bet yours will be superglad to see you. They must have missed their only daughter."

Outside, the dry desert air hit me like a blast from a hair dryer, and the sunshine made me blink. Tomorrow I'd be home in Massachusetts, where the forecast was cloudy and humid.

Along with most of the other campers, Emma, Olivia,

and Lucy were sprawled on the oval-shaped lawn in front of the nurse's office. Emma spotted me first and waved. "Where *were* you?"

Olivia sat up and tugged her hat to shade her face. "We thought you were dead."

"Wait." Lucy looked around. "Are you just getting here?"

Emma rolled her eyes. "Yeah, she's just getting here. Where did you think—?"

"—I dunno." Lucy shrugged. "Over with Vivek or something."

"Leave me alone about Vivek," I said.

Lucy said, "Okay," but Olivia said, "Sor-*ree*!" and Emma asked, "Grace, are you okay? Do you want a glass of water?"

"She's gonna miss Vivek," Lucy said.

"Will you please *stop*—" I started to say, but then, with no warning, I burst into tears.

There was a surprised pause, followed quickly by a collective cooing sound—*oh-h-h-h*—followed quickly by a group hug. I closed my eyes, feeling better because my friends loved me and worse because I was about to lose them forever.

"Excuse me. Grace?" The voice was muffled but familiar. "Is that you? And are these the girls about whom you speak so often?"

Oh no. I should have remembered another embarrassing thing about my parents: They are always early.

CHAPTER 4

Grace

I introduced my parents to the Flowerpot girls, who were friendly even though they must have been in shock about how my parents' outfits *practically matched*: Khakis, polos, and loafers all around, except my father's polo was baby blue and my mother's was pink.

Then my parents wanted to put my trunk in the car and leave. Once they had seen that my friends were clean with no visible tattoos, that was all they needed to know. My parents don't really believe in small talk.

But Hannah—who could earn a gold medal in small talk with grown-ups if there were such a thing—explained that parents' staying for lunch is traditional, and after that mine settled down because tradition is something they understand.

My dad, Joe Xi, was born and raised in Singapore, where his family still lives. My mom's name is Anna Burrows, and she grew up all over the world because her dad was in the U.S. government. They met in college in Massachusetts, and now they are both very brainy scientists, the kind who expect their only daughter to be brainy too.

Olivia's parents arrived next. They are tall and glamorous and African-American, and they look just like their picture on the bottles of Baron Barbecue Sauce you see in every supermarket. Also, they were dressed exactly right for picking up their daughter at summer camp in Arizona—jeans and a polo for him, jeans skirt, a T-shirt, and a turquoise necklace for her. Like movie stars, they smiled a lot. Unlike movie stars—my idea of them anyway—they also gave everybody big warm hugs.

Emma's parents turned out to be huggers, too, and the second they saw her they glued themselves to Emma like they'd never again let her out of their sight. Emma's dad is a doctor, I remembered, and her mom is a lawyer. For parents they are kind of old—almost grandparent-age. I liked them, though, and anyway you would never call them embarrassing. Here is something cute: They were holding hands.

After that it was time for lunch, and Lucy's mom still wasn't there.

All of us could see Lucy was unhappy, and I thought she was worried something might have happened to her mom. But it turned out she was mad.

"You never get mad," Emma said. We were in the dining hall by then, filling water glasses to carry back to our table for the grown-ups.

Lucy said, "At my mom I do."

Emma looked over her shoulder at me, and I shrugged. We knew Lucy lived with her mom and her grandma in Beverly Hills. We knew Lucy's family didn't have a lot of money. We knew Lucy's aunt Freda had been a camper at Moonlight Ranch when she was a kid.

We didn't know anything else.

"I'll carry your mom's water," Lucy told me, "so I have something—" She stopped in her tracks. "Oh, no."

All of us stopped too, and looked where she was looking. A woman had appeared by the door. She had a lot of blond hair and a big smile, but the most remarkable thing was what she was wearing—a sleeveless green blouse, the shortest shorts I ever saw on a grown-up, and green cowboy boots.

Olivia started to say something, and from her face I knew it would be snarky. But Emma kicked her and then said, "That's not your mom, Lucy. Say it's not."

Lucy sighed, looked into each of our faces like she was going to her own execution, then turned and started walking toward the blond woman, waving. "I'm over here, Mother!"

Am I mean if I felt better after Lucy's mom turned out to be even more embarrassing than my parents?

Her name was Karen Kathleen, but she went by KK,

and even though she was wearing those terrible shorts, she was nice—friendly—and she made everybody laugh, even my own mom.

Lunch was the regular camp food—hamburgers and salad. There were veggie burgers for vegetarians like Lucy and her mom. While we ate, Hannah told stories about the summer—like how Flowerpot Cabin should've won first prize on Talent Night, only there was that Ryan kid in Lasso Cabin who had an international trophy in violin, so even though the other boys only tapped on spoons from the dining hall, their band still won.

Vivek was in Lasso Cabin. Of the three spoon players, he was the best. Now he was sitting two tables away with his parents, and I was carefully looking in the opposite direction.

"And didn't you girls make cookies?" Emma's mom asked.

"From my grandfather's recipe," Hannah said. "They were delicious. These daughters of yours can really bake."

"Vivek was there too, and we sent some to his mom for her birthday," Olivia said, looking at me. "Where is Vivek anyway? I want to talk to his mom. I want to know if she liked the cookies."

But before Olivia had a chance to look around, Buck, the head of camp, rang the cowbell to get everybody's attention.

"I just wanted to say a few words about what wonderful kids y'all have and what a pleasure it's been . . ."

You get the idea.

We were pushing our chairs back when Hannah said, "Would you parents mind if I borrowed your daughters one last time? You'll want to go out and open up your cars and get the AC going. Otherwise you'll roast."

Since no cars are allowed in camp, parking is out beyond the fence. Now we Flowerpot girls gathered for the last time under the cottonwood by the front gate.

Hannah's eyes looked damp, but she spoke briskly. "Good-byes should be short and sweet. But I did want to give you each something."

From her day pack she pulled four small presents,

each wrapped in newspaper and rainbow ribbons, each marked with our own name.

Olivia shook her head sadly. "Such a *shame* you couldn't get real wrapping paper."

"Newspaper's good because it's recycled," said Lucy.

"Let's open them, everybody!" said Emma.

Inside were recipe boxes—a green one for Lucy, pink for Olivia, red for me, and blue for Emma. There were recipes inside, too—cookie recipes.

"Your grandfather's?" Emma asked.

Hannah nodded, and by now a couple of tears had escaped her eyes. "There's a baker's dozen there, his thirteen all-time favorites."

"A dozen is twelve, Hannah," said Lucy.

"A baker's dozen is thirteen," Hannah explained, "and I am gonna miss you guys. Now, get out of here! Short and sweet, remember? But don't forget me ... and don't forget each other!"

To help me find it, my parents had told me their rental car was a red Ford. But it turned out so was everyone else's—except Olivia's family's. The Barons had a gold Porsche SUV that stood out by a mile as it drove past. The windows were tinted so I couldn't see O, but I waved anyway. I was still looking for my parents when someone behind me called, "Grace! Hang on!"

It was Vivek, and I felt myself turn bright red from embarrassment . . . and maybe happiness, a little. I turned around, and he was two feet away from me holding out a small brown paper sack stamped MOONLIGHT RANCH TRADING POST.

"I bought these for you. I mean, not for you exactly. But they made a, uh . . . mistake and gave me these. And everyone likes them, so you must like them too. Here."

I took the sack, too surprised to look inside right away, and then my parents came up.

"Who is this, Grace?" asked my father.

I introduced Vivek, who smiled and held out his hand. "My parents—" He looked around, but the sound of a car horn drowned out his voice. It was Lucy's mom honking as she drove by. Lucy didn't wave. She was too busy gesturing to her mom: *Please quiet down!*

Vivek and I locked eyes for about half a second. Then I said, "We have to go. Have a really great year." And I pulled my parents away.

In the car, I stowed the sack in my day pack without looking inside. What if it was a big disappointment? What if anticipation was the best part?

Better to save the secret for later.

Since our flight to Boston was at six the next morning, we were staying in a very nice, very clean hotel by the airport. Usually I don't notice if hotels are nice or not, but after six weeks of sharing a room with four other people and sleeping in an upper bunk that squeaked, I definitely noticed. Likewise the air conditioning and the amazing menu at the hotel restaurant.

Now that we were alone, my parents weren't embarrassing anymore. Moonlight Ranch might've been the best thing that ever happened to me, but still . . . I had missed them.

My parents and I read in the room after dinner. Right before it was time to turn out the light, I took the paper sack into the bathroom. I counted to ten. I looked inside. I laughed.

"Are you okay, Grace?" my mother called.

"Yeah, fine." I flushed the toilet for show, came out, and zipped the sack into an inside pocket of my suitcase. My parents did not notice.

"We have been saving some news for you," my mother said.

My bed was beside theirs. The air conditioning was so chilly, I had to pull up the covers. "What?"

"You have been promoted to sixth grade—you are skipping fifth!" said my dad. "It is all arranged with your school and your teachers. Congratulations!"

CHAPTER 5

Grace

Sixth grade at Nashoba Elementary was terrible but not unbearable, and after a while I began to rate the days. They were either excellent (when I did well on an assignment, there were Oreos in my lunch, and no one bothered me), good (when I did well on an assignment and no one bothered me), or bad (when someone teased me).

Then I had to add a new rating: disastrous.

This happened on a Thursday in October that had

started out fine. I got 100 percent on the spelling test, raised my hand and correctly answered a question about world geography (River Nile), and filled in a worksheet on how plants make energy from sunlight. After lunch, Mrs. Keeran, our teacher, announced it was time to talk about the field trip to Walden Pond, which "will offer a unique opportunity to study history, literature, philosophy, and biology."

My classmates looked bored, but they might have just been busy digesting their lunches. I was looking forward to the field trip. It would be a whole day spent outside room 111, a whole day of sun and sky and water and trees.

"As you know, class," Mrs. Keeran continued, "you will work in pairs both at the pond and afterward on your Walden projects."

Even though I had no friends in room 111, I wasn't worried about working in pairs. The class had done two other pair projects, and both times I had been with Kelly, who is even quieter than me. Kelly and I had developed a good system. My job was to do everything, and hers was to look anxious about how I was doing it but never complain.

But this time, Mrs. Keeran said, we weren't going to get to pick our own partners. This time she would assign them, and before I even knew what was happening, she had read all our names off the attendance book, and I was partnered with Shoshi Rubinstein!

My stomach lurched. Shoshi, two seats behind me, groaned loudly. And after that, a couple of her minions began to giggle.

CHAPTER 6

Grace

On Thursdays, I have ballet after school, and after that Lily's dad drops me off at my house. Lily lives in my neighborhood and she's in my ballet class, and we used to be friends. But now that I skipped a grade, it feels awkward, and besides, we only see each other at ballet.

"Thanks, Mr. Stone. Bye, Lily." I closed the car door and then went to the mailbox at the foot of our driveway, took out the mail, and jogged up our front walk.

Since Mrs. Keeran had paired me with Shoshi Rubinstein, my stomach hadn't stopped hurting. I had gotten through ballet, though, and provided I didn't eat dinner, I'd probably be okay. The next day I would work up the nerve to beg Mrs. Keeran to give me Kelly as a partner as usual. It's not as if Shoshi wanted to work with me. She would prefer one of her minions so together they could giggle and plot mean-girl plots.

Usually the mail is two or three catalogs no one looks at and an equal number of envelopes no one opens. About once a month there's a blue air mail envelope with Singaporean stamps on it. This is from "home," as my father calls it, sent by my grandmother or an old auntie who doesn't use Skype. The letters say who is in the hospital or getting divorced or getting married or having a baby or dead. They are always long, and my father makes me sit down and listen to them read out loud.

I tossed the mail on the kitchen island the way I always do. There was no letter from Singapore, but there was one that was strange—square and addressed in purple ink. I glanced at that one again and saw something really strange: It was addressed to me!

Instead of opening it right away, I examined it for clues. The writing was round and neat. There was no return address, but the postmark was Los Angeles, 90035.

I didn't know anyone in Los Angeles.

When I flipped the envelope over, I saw it was sealed with three glitter stickers: a dolphin, a unicorn, and a rainbow.

And all at once I remembered—and I tore the envelope open, pulled out the pages (which were purple with pink lines and smelled like lavender soap), and read, without even taking off my heavy school backpack or sitting down.

Saturday, October 10

Hi Grace!

I am not going to write "How are you? I am fine" because that is what everybody always writes. Right?

So . . . what have you been up to since camp? I mean besides school. I like art class with Mrs. Coatrak, but otherwise school is always boring and always the same, right?

At camp, I didn't think I'd be that busy this year, but I am because guess what? I am babysitting for triplets who live on our street!

The triplets are almost four and here are their names: Arlo, Mia, and Levi. Arlo likes animals, Mia likes games, and Levi likes to play pretend.

Kendall, the mom, is also there when I babysit. I am supposed to keep the triplets safe and play with them so that she, Kendall, does not go totally bonkers being a mom.

The first day I babysat them, Arlo stomped an anthill to destroy it. I yelled at him because ants are living

creatures. Then the ants started biting
Arlo, and he started crying, and soon
all three of them were freaking out. I
think I almost got fired the very first
day, but now it's getting better.

My nana says I am now the breadwinner
in our family. She is kidding but also
not, because it's true at the moment
I am the only one in my family with a
job. (My mom is looking for one, though.
I think she was hoping we would soon be
moving in with her boyfriend, but that
didn't happen, and I think now she is
looking for a new boyfriend, too.)

My nana is my grandmother. Maybe I
never told you that before. My mom and I
live with her in her house.

Change of topic. ("Change of topic" is
something my mom says, usually when
things get hairy and she's afraid Nana
might leave the room or yell.) Does

Moonlight Ranch seem like it was a long time ago to you? Do you think about it and me and Olivia and Emma?

Now you have to write back. Maybe you noticed at camp that I am the only kid in the universe who doesn't have her own phone. Also I am the only kid who doesn't have a laptop or a tablet or even a computer at her house. My nana says electronics are sapping our brainpower and turning us into a nation of empty-headed twits. I am not telling you this to be pathetic (honest!!!) but to explain that you can't text me or message me or e-mail me like you would a normal person. You will have to write me a letter. But then it will all be worthwhile because after I get it YOU WILL GET COOKIES!!!

Love ya always,
Lucy

P.S. I saw you and Vivek saying good-bye on the last day of camp. Did he give you a present? You can tell me. I would never blab!

CHAPTER 7

Grace

As I read, I answered Lucy's questions in my head:

Yes, Moonlight Ranch seemed like a long time ago.

Yes, I was busy.

No, I didn't think about Lucy, Emma, and Olivia very much.

(And if sometimes I thought about Vivek, I would never tell.)

Most of all, Lucy's letter reminded me that I did have

friends. This made me feel so much better after my disaster day that I decided to read it again. My stomach wasn't in a knot anymore, so I went to the cupboard, got out three Oreos, and ate them. Then I sat down in the plaid recliner in the family room, and put the letter in my lap. I was just going to close my eyes for a second before I re-read it, but the next thing I knew, my father's hand was shaking my shoulder.

"Gracie? Are you sick? What's wrong?"

"I got this letter." I held it up as if it explained everything. "It's from Lucy."

"You should go to bed early tonight," my father said.

I shook my head and yawned. "I have to get ready for Mr. Sterling tomorrow"—Mr. Sterling is my math tutor—"and I have to practice piano and do vocabulary building."

"Have you eaten?" Dad asked.

"Uh . . . some carrots? After school." It's true that the carrots were really Oreos, but my father didn't need to know that.

"You will never get big on carrots," Dad said. "Let me

microwave something, and we'll eat together. I think, for once, it would not kill you to skip a day of piano practice."

I took my backpack up to my room, then went into the bathroom and splashed cold water on my face. When I came back downstairs, I could smell tomato sauce, and my dad was serving squares of something with bubbling cheese on top.

"Eggplant parmesan." My father shrugged. "Its label reported the highest calorie count of any of the boxes in the freezer."

We sat at the island and ate together. The food was salty and a little slimy, but I was hungry and my stomach remained calm. While we were eating, Mom came home. Usually, I am practicing piano when she comes in, and Dad spoke before she had a chance to.

"Grace is taking a break from piano for today," he said. "We are not going to discuss it. And she has had a lovely letter from Lucy at camp. You remember Lucy?"

My mother would never contradict my father in front

of me, so she only raised her eyebrows about piano. Then she said, "Lucy's mother was the one wearing shorts and boots?"

"That's the one." My father nodded.

If both my parents remembered Lucy's mom's clothes, did everyone else remember how my parents had matched?

Loyally, I said, "Lucy's mother is pretty."

My mother's response was to ask how Lucy was doing in school, and I told her Lucy was babysitting.

By this time my mother had made herself a cup of tea and sat down with my dad and me. "It's too bad Lucy has to work when she could be taking music lessons or something," she said.

Once when I was little I saw a show on Disney where a grandmother character called her granddaughter a "snot-nosed brat." I was shocked! My family would never use words like that. But at the same time, it gave a name to the part of me that sometimes wants to be bad: Snot-Nosed Grace.

Now Snot-Nosed Grace spoke up: "I think I would

like to work. I would like to have money of my own."

As expected, my parents' response was immediate. "Don't we give you anything you want?" my dad asked.

"You don't need money," my mother said.

"But," my father added, "we must not judge the ideas of other families. We don't know everything."

"Don't we?" my mom asked, and I thought maybe she was serious, but then she winked at my dad, and they laughed . . . and so did I.

CHAPTER 8

Grace

Friday counted as an okay day at school. We were supposed to meet for the first time in our Walden pairs, but—luckily—art cleanup went too long and then the school day was over. I had time before chess club and could have asked Mrs. Keeran to change out Shoshi for Kelly then, but I lost my nerve. I promised myself I would do it on Monday.

It was the next morning, Saturday, that I sat down

at my desk to write to Lucy and felt bad that I didn't
have fragrant purple stationery or stickers or a pink pen
or anything fun the way she did. All I had was regular
lined notebook paper and a blue Bic pen. I hoped Lucy
wouldn't mind.

Saturday, October 17

Dear Lucy,
   Thank you very much for your nice letter.
Please forgive me for not replying sooner.
You are right that I am busy. But what I
am busy with is more boring than babysitting
for Arlo, Mia, and Levi. (Please give them
my regards.)
   You said you think I must have lots of
friends here, but I do not. What I do have
is one enemy. Her name is Shoshi Rubinstein,
and she is in my class at school, and she
hates me. I did not do anything to make her
hate me, except she also takes ballet with

me, and Mademoiselle G, our teacher, told me
I have nice posture on the same day she told
Shoshi to stop slouching.

Shoshi is unusually tall. I cannot help that.
Can I?

So now Shoshi and her tall, slouchy friends
giggle and whisper when I walk by, and I
think they have a bad nickname for me, too,
but I don't know what it is. I think Shoshi
is a mean girl (we learned about them in our
anti-bullying unit), and I have noticed that
mean girls always have lots of friends. Have
you noticed this too? They clump together
like lint.

Change of topic. :^)

I think I would like to have a job and
to be in charge of something like you are
in charge of Arlo, Mia, and Levi. Do you
supervise their games? Do you speak to them
in a foreign language, and if so, which one?
Do you encourage them to exercise so they

will have strong muscles and healthy hearts?

Here are the answers to your questions.

Yes, we are still friends. In fact, you are one of my only friends and you are 2,983 miles away. (I looked it up.)

Now that you have reminded me, I miss my bunkmates at camp and Hannah, too.

Thank you for remembering the Secret Cookie Club. But if you are too busy, you do not have to make me any cookies. I do not want to put you to any trouble. It is enough that you thought of me and wrote a nice letter.

Sincerely, Your Friend Grace Xi

P.S. If you are making Hannah's grandpa's chocolate chip cookies, I would like pecans in them.

P.P.S. What Vivek gave me was not serious.

When I read my letter over, I thought of crossing out the part about lint because it was definitely Snot-Nosed Grace talking, and would Lucy realize when she read it that I am not really the nice person she thinks I am? It was too bad we couldn't talk the way we used to after lights-out, but Lucy hadn't even given me a phone number, and when I checked the camp directory that Moonlight Ranch gave to our family at the end of the summer, there wasn't a phone number there either— only an address. How strange.

In fact, Lucy seemed so far away (well, she was) and her life so different from mine that I couldn't imagine it. She might as well live in a grass shack on a street made of sand in a village surrounded by palm trees.

CHAPTER 9

Grace

After the flag salute Monday morning, Mrs. Keeran announced we would absolutely be meeting in our Walden pairs that afternoon. So, when the bell rang for lunch, I went up to her desk.

"Yes, Grace? What can I do for you?" Mrs. Keeran is the only African-American teacher at my school. She almost always wears her long hair pulled back and a pair of beaded clip-on earrings that match her outfit.

Today they were magenta to match the roses on her cardigan.

I had practiced what I was going to say in bed the night before. "Hi, Mrs. Keeran. Would it be okay if you changed it so I am Kelly's partner for the Walden project instead of Shoshanna's? I am sure Shoshanna wouldn't mind."

Shoshanna is Shoshi's real name. No one calls her that, but I did because I was making a formal request.

"Ri-i-i-ight," Mrs. Keeran said. "And why is it you'd like me to do that?"

I wasn't prepared for that question. For a moment, I stared at a Massachusetts wildlife photograph on the bulletin board behind Mrs. Keeran's desk. It showed a black bear about to tackle a beehive. I had seen the picture every day since school started but never thought about it till now. Would the honey be worth all those stings?

"Grace?" Mrs. Keeran said.

"Because I hate Shoshi," I answered, and then I felt

my face flush. Why had I said that? It was the fault of the picture—it distracted me!

"Hate is a strong word," said Mrs. Keeran.

"Not hate," I said quickly. "I mean, Shoshi and I . . . we are not compatible."

Mrs. Keeran nodded. "I've noticed some tension between the two of you. But may I tell you something in confidence? Before you skipped a grade, Shoshanna was usually the best student in the class. I think it's been hard on her having you here."

I looked at my toes. Hard on Shoshi? What about hard on me when she whispers behind my back?

"So I thought perhaps," Mrs. Keeran went on, "if you worked together and got to know each other, you'd learn to like each other. You're both hardworking and serious about your studies. You both take ballet. And if you can't learn to *like* each other"—Mrs. Keeran must've noticed me frowning—"at least you could learn to practice tolerance."

"*Please* can you switch us, Mrs. Keeran?" I knew I sounded babyish, but I was desperate.

Mrs. Keeran set her jaw. "Let's give my way a try, shall we?" she said. "If you and Shoshi really can't get along at all during the planning, we'll see what we can do about changing partners before the field trip."

Grace

As of lunchtime that day, what I knew about Shoshi Rubinstein were pretty much the same things anybody else in my class would know:

(1) She wears a bra! (2) She has one older brother and one older sister. (3) She almost never wears the same outfit twice. (4) She lives in my neighborhood in a green house with white trim. (5) She has a collie dog that barks. (6) She is bad at dance but her

parents make her go. (7) She hates me for no reason.

By the time the bell rang after school, I had learned four more things: (8) She is bossy. (9) She likes using pink gel pens for notes. (10) She thinks she has artistic talent. (11) When she's mad, she yells.

I found those four things out at the first Walden meeting, which happened in the library because it's easier to work together at long tables than little desks. Mrs. Keeran had handed out a homework assignment due next week, and we were supposed to divide up responsibilities for it, then start work. It was the only class time she was giving us, so if we didn't finish, we would have to find time to meet on our own.

You can imagine the knot in my stomach when I looked up to see Shoshi stomping toward me at the table where I had sat down. The table was by the window, I guess in case I needed to jump out of it for any reason. When Shoshi sat down, she dropped her pink zebra-striped backpack on the table, and it landed with a *thump*.

Probably I am making Shoshi sound like Godzilla,

which is not 100 percent fair. Some people (not me) might even think she was pretty. She has straight light brown hair, a small nose, and green eyes. On her jaw there is a mole like a squashed flea.

"Okay, we have to work together, so let's get this over with." Shoshi pulled her notebook out of her backpack along with a pink gel pen.

I didn't say anything.

"Cat got your tongue?" she asked.

"What? No," I said.

"Do you agree we should get this over with?"

"Yes."

"Good," said Shoshi. "So what's going to happen is you find the ten facts and write them and then I do the illustrations for them. I'm good at art. Later this week, you e-mail me the facts you find, and if they're okay, then I'll start my part."

If I had said, "Okay," the meeting would've been over, which would've been good. But it was irritating to be told what to do. I could feel Snot-Nosed Grace wanting to speak up, but I tried to keep my voice normal.

"No," I said. "You do five facts and illustrate them, and so will I. Then we'll read each other's to make sure they're okay."

Shoshi scowled. "My way's better because I'm good at art."

Besides Snot-Nosed Grace, there is something else about me that isn't entirely nice. Sometimes I have a bad temper. Most of the time it doesn't show because most of the time I am not arguing with anybody, but now I felt my temper building like steam in a teakettle. To cool it down, I took a breath. "No," I said. "My way's better because it's more fair."

Shoshi tipped her chair back and shook her head. "You really do think you're smarter than everyone else, don't you? Well, you're not."

Now my temper burst out in a squawk. "I never said I was!"

"*And* you're stuck-up."

"Oh yeah? Well, you're a bully."

"You're a runt."

"At least I don't slouch."

By this time everyone from room 111 was staring, and Mrs. Collins the librarian was striding toward us. "*Girls!* What has gotten into you?"

Shoshi jumped up. *"She started it!"*

And then I was on my feet too. *"No, I didn't—she did!"*

CHAPTER 11

Grace

The principal of my school is Mrs. Lila Barnes. Her short gray hair and black-rimmed glasses make her look serious, but for holidays she wears ugly sweaters, and sometimes for no reason she wears a light-up headband or pink high-tops covered in sequins.

It was 2:56 p.m. when Shoshi and I arrived in her office. There were only ten minutes left till the first bus bell, and Mrs. Barnes probably didn't expect new discipline problems that day.

I'm sure she didn't expect Shoshi and me.

"I trust you two can take the long walk to Mrs. Barnes's office together without further incident," Mrs. Collins had said. "Now go."

And we did, me walking a couple of steps behind Shoshi, neither of us saying anything.

In the outer office, the school secretary told us to take a seat and wait. By this time, my temper had turned from hot steam to icy dread. The wait was probably only two minutes, but it was the longest two minutes of my life. I had never been in trouble before. My stomach was tied in a knot.

Of course Shoshi did not deserve any sympathy. But I did wonder a little bit if she might be feeling the same. She was sitting right here next to me, both of us here for the same reason. In a strange way, we were bound together.

The door to Mrs. Barnes's inner office opened, and she looked out at us, sitting side by side. "Come in, young ladies."

We went, and Mrs. Barnes gestured at two orange plastic chairs across from her desk. We both sat down. The seat felt hard and uncomfortable.

"Shouting in the library? Calling each other names?" Mrs. Barnes shook her head sadly. "That's what Mrs. Collins said when she phoned. I am all ears if you would like to tell me your versions. Shoshanna?"

"What Mrs. Collins said is right, Mrs. Barnes," Shoshi said in a voice so low it didn't even sound like hers. "I'm sorry."

"Grace?" Mrs. Barnes looked at me.

"I'm sorry too," I said.

"And what was this disagreement about?" Mrs. Barnes asked.

I spoke first. "Mrs. Keeran assigned us to be partners on the Walden project, and Shoshi was telling me what to do, and—"

"—That's not right," Shoshi interrupted. "The assignment was to divide responsibilities, and we were dividing responsibilities, and then Grace started yelling."

"I did not yell. But if I did, it was because you were bossing me," I said.

"Because you were being uncooperative," Shoshi said.

"Because your idea was bad," I said.

"It was *not*!"

"It was *too*!"

"Young ladies?" Mrs. Barnes raised one hand like a traffic cop. "What I am hearing is that you disagreed over how to approach the Walden project, and then the disagreement escalated, and you both lost your tempers. Is that about right?"

After a pause we answered at the same time: "I guess," I said. "Basically," Shoshi said.

Mrs. Barnes laid her palms on her desk, leaned forward, and looked from Shoshi to me. "Is it ever appropriate to yell in the library?"

"No," we said.

"Is it ever helpful to call people names?"

"No," we said again.

"All right, then." Mrs. Barnes leaned back in her chair. "You seem to be sorry, but you did disrupt class. Because of that, I am giving you each one after-school detention. I know you both have ballet, so we'll say Wednesday in room 213."

Mrs. Barnes stood up after that, which was the signal for us to leave.

"Are you going to call our parents?" I asked.

"Yes, Grace," she said. "They need to plan for picking you up after detention."

"Mine won't care," Shoshi said. "I walk home from school anyway."

"You do?" The words slipped out because I was surprised.

Shoshi shrugged and looked at me sideways. "Yeah. So what?"

"Be that as it may"—Mrs. Barnes opened the door for us—"your parents will get phone calls."

CHAPTER 12

Grace

On Mondays after school, the blue Music Academy van picks me up to take me for my piano lesson. When that's over, I stay there and do homework in the study room until my mom can leave work and come to get me.

If the two minutes outside Mrs. Barnes's office were long, the time waiting for my mom that afternoon was eternal. I couldn't even concentrate on decimals.

Would Mrs. Barnes have called her already?

My parents had never been mad at me before. They didn't even know about Snot-Nosed Grace. I had always managed to keep her existence a secret.

Finally, my mom drove up in our white SUV. When she didn't turn her head to look at me, I knew Mrs. Barnes had talked to her already. Trying not to think about anything, I opened the rear door and threw in my backpack the way I always do, closed the door, opened the front, and slid in. Because I'm small, I'd had to ride in the backseat longer than any of my friends. Now I wished I could crawl back there again and hide out.

My door had barely closed when my mom spoke, still looking straight ahead. "We are not going to talk about this now. We are going to talk about it as a family when your father gets home."

Most Mondays I stay downstairs and do homework at the kitchen island. That day I went upstairs to my bedroom.

My parents started decorating my bedroom on the same day the ultrasound told them I was a girl. It is pale pink with a border of wallpaper printed in pink roses. My curtains match the wallpaper. On the walls, my parents hung framed posters of paintings of children by important artists: Mary Cassatt, Pierre-Auguste Renoir, and John Singer Sargent.

I have a canopy bed with a white lace cover, a white desk for my computer, and a white rocking chair with a pink gingham pillow. My bookcase is full of hardcover books by Charles Dickens, Louisa May Alcott, L. M. Montgomery, and Laura Ingalls Wilder.

Almost the only things in my room I chose myself are the bulletin board over my desk and what's tacked to it: a picture of a boy band I used to like, a picture of my parents from their university days, a Dora the Explorer valentine from my second-grade boyfriend, Nino, and a fortune from a fortune cookie that reads: "You will excel at everything you do."

The most recent thing added to the bulletin board is the official Moonlight Ranch camp photograph. It was taken at the gymkhana corral. I'm standing in the first row middle because I'm short, with Lucy (tall), Emma (taller), and Olivia (tallest) like stair steps next to me. Vivek is sitting on the fence on the end, looking off to the left, distracted.

I studied Vivek's cute face for a moment and then I pulled open the bottom drawer of my desk. It was empty except for one thing—a paper sack from the Moonlight Ranch Trading Post. I didn't bother to look inside. I knew what was there, and even on this bad day it made me smile.

I still had homework to do that afternoon, but I decided to unclutter my bulletin board instead. I didn't even like that boy band anymore, so I yanked off the picture and threw it away. Then I did the same with the valentine from Nino. He moved back to the Philippines in third grade. Why had I even left it up there that long?

After that, I stuck my hands in my pockets and walked in squares around my room—seven paces, pivot, seven paces, pivot, seven paces. . . . Then I was afraid I might make my leg muscles lopsided, so I reversed and walked in the other direction—seven paces, pivot. . . .

There is a limit to how much worrying you can do

about a single thing. After a few laps, my mind wandered to Shoshi and to the amazing fact that she walks home from school.

Our town is safe, and the school is only a mile from our neighborhood. Even so, my parents would never let me walk by myself. The idea that one of my classmates did it every day was part thrilling and part scary. It reminded me of finding out that Lucy in Los Angeles didn't have a phone or a computer. All along, I thought I was the normal one, but maybe it was me who lived a life like nobody else's, me who lived in a grass hut among palm trees.

When you are an only child, you know your parents very well. This was a new situation—me being in trouble—but still I could predict some things about what my parents would do. One was that my mom would want my dad to do the talking.

"Is this true what Mrs. Barnes told your mother?" he asked. It was evening by this time, and we were in the living room, which normally is used only when there are guests. My parents were in the two arm-chairs by the coffee table, and I was on the love seat across from them, perched on the edge like a bird that might take off.

I told him yes, and then I explained what happened, and then they looked at each other, and then my father looked at me again. "Do you want us to telephone the other girl's parents?" he asked. "Perhaps if she explained to Mrs. Barnes that she was at fault after all—"

I was horrified. "What—*no*!"

"Then I don't understand," my father said. "You are at fault?"

My parents grew up going to private schools—my father in Singapore, my mother all over the world. What did they know about a partner project at a public school in Massachusetts, USA? I could talk all day, but I'd never be able to explain it to them.

"It isn't like that," I said miserably. "You don't understand."

"We are attempting to," said my father.

I took a breath and tried again. "I shouldn't have

yelled in the library. I probably deserve to be in trouble, but so does Shoshi. And the worst part is we still have to work together on the Walden project . . . that is, unless Mrs. Keeran decides to give us a break and let us pick new partners."

"Do you want me to telephone Mrs.—"

"No!" I interrupted again.

My mother shook her head. "This isn't like you."

I looked at the ceiling, at my toes, and then out the window before looking back at my parents. "Thank you for trying to help," I said, "but I would be embarrassed if you called either Shoshi's parents or Mrs. Keeran. I'm not a little kid anymore. Some things I have to do myself."

When my parents glanced at each other for the second time, I hoped maybe the conversation was done . . . but that would have been too easy. Of course, there had to be a lecture, too: "We are disappointed in you, Grace," my father said. "Because you have many natural gifts, our expectations for you are high. At the same time, this world is competitive, and you can't afford slipups if you are going to succeed. This was a slipup, but we still have confidence you will do what's right and make us proud of you again."

I hated that I had disappointed them and blinked back a tear. "Okay," I said in my tiniest voice.

Then my mother said, "How about some soup for dinner? I can heat up that Campbell's kind you like."

CHAPTER 13

Grace

Mrs. Keeran sometimes e-mails reminders about assignments. I never before forgot an assignment, but today had been a day of never-befores, so at bedtime I checked. There were no e-mails from Mrs. Keeran, but I did have a message from Shoshi.

I didn't want to open it. It might say something mean.

Then I gave a lecture to myself: Grace Xi, stop this wimpiness right now.

And then I opened the e-mail:

hey, so fine. you do 5 facts and i will too and we get our own images or draw pictures or whatever. only you have to come over so we can work on it since we didn't work today in library. when can you come over?

Bossy as ever, I thought. Why did we have to work at *her* house? What was the matter with *my* house?

I almost e-mailed back that exactly, but then decided to wait. Spitting out toothpaste and pulling on pajamas, I thought some more. She had compromised on how we were going to do the assignment. So maybe I could compromise too?

The idea of doing anything Shoshi's way was very irritating. And here is something else irritating: She didn't use capital letters in her e-mail.

The door to my parents' room was open, and the light was still on, so I went in to say good night. As usual, they were in bed reading. I kissed first my mom and then my dad on the cheek, inhaling their familiar soap-and-toothpaste smells.

"I love you," I told them.

"We love you, Grace," my father said.

"Yes," said my mother, "but no more nonsense at school please."

The next morning I went up to Shoshi's desk before the first bell rang. I wanted to get it over with. I said it was okay if we worked at her house, and she told me (still bossy!) to come on Friday, and I said no because of chess club. After that no other day worked either—we had ballet on Tuesday and Thursday, detention on Wednesday.

While we were talking, Shoshi's minions were arriving. It is Snot-Nosed Grace who calls them Shoshi's minions. Their real names are Deirdre and Nell, and they both sit with Shoshi at lunch every day and they even dress like her. Today's approved outfit was leggings, skirts, and pullover sweaters with Keds.

(I was wearing a navy polo and pink khakis with Keds.)

Now they both sat down at their desks and got out their binders, and then they looked at me talking to Shoshi, and they whispered to each other and smirked.

Whatever, minions.

"Saturday afternoon, then," Shoshi said. "Two o'clock."

I didn't want it to look like I was obeying a command or something, so I shrugged very casually. "Okay, I guess."

On Wednesday afternoon I found out what detention is like at Nashoba Elementary School. What happens is this. You go upstairs to room 213. Mr. Long, the fourth-grade teacher, asks you to sign a piece of paper on a clipboard so the school can keep track that you showed up. He smiles sympathetically even though he doesn't really know you, which makes you feel about one-tenth of one percent less totally humiliated.

Then you sit down at a desk and look around at the six other people who are in trouble, and you notice they're all boys but for you and Shoshi.

You know Thomas Pendleton was tardy three days in a row, and Chris Bigler (he's always in trouble) used a bad word where a playground monitor could hear him. But you don't know what the other boys are in for, and you wonder if it's worse than what you and Shoshi did.

Shoshi, by the way, is sitting in the front of the classroom and hasn't looked at you once.

The classroom is really quiet, and at first you feel kind of awful. You think about how you don't want to be there but you're not allowed to leave, which means you are trapped, and you imagine a jail breakout like on TV.

But after a few moments you give up and do your homework for a while . . . and then it's over.

Thursday and Friday that week rated okay. Thursday might even have been "good" (I got 100 on the map quiz plus two extra-credit points for identifying oranges as Florida's most valuable agricultural product, no Oreos though), except that in the back of my head was the worry about having to go to Shoshi's house.

CHAPTER 14

Grace

On Saturday morning I have Chinese class and after that karate.

Lily from ballet is also in karate, and my parents take her home.

"What are you doing this afternoon?" Lily asked me in the car. "I'm going to Rose Ellen's birthday party."

Rose Ellen is someone we both know from our class last year. If I hadn't skipped a grade, I would have been going to her birthday party too.

"I'm going to Shoshi Rubinstein's to work on the Walden project," I said. "She's my partner."

Lily's eyes got big. "Poor you! You hate Shoshi Rubinstein! Didn't Mrs. Keeran know that?"

"Who is it Grace hates?" my mother asked from the front seat. Lily and I were both sitting in the back.

"You already know I don't get along with Shoshi, Mom. We are working on it."

I saw my mother's frown in the rearview mirror. "I hope so."

Lily scrunched her face and mouthed a silent, exaggerated, *"Sorry."*

Lunch was macaroni and cheese from the black and purple box, which my parents believe is superior to the kind in the blue and orange box. I ate two helpings along with an apple and a glass of milk. I needed strength because I was planning to ask my parents for permission to do something shocking and unheard of. I wanted to ride my bike to Shoshi's house by myself.

While I ate, I organized my arguments: (1) It is only four blocks. (2) The last crime in my neighborhood was in the summer when Mr. Bigler (Chris Bigler's father; misbehavior must run in that family) didn't pick up after their dog, and the last crime before that no one wrote down because the Pilgrims hadn't arrived yet. (3) Even though it is only four blocks, riding my bike is still good exercise. (4) Because I am never allowed to go anywhere, my bike gathers dust in the garage, which is wasteful. (5) Some kids (Shoshi) walk all the way to school without a grown-up, and that's much farther, and she has never been kidnapped or run over by a car.

I was putting my plate in the dishwasher when my mother came into the kitchen and asked, "What time do you want me to take you to Shoshi's house?"

"You don't have to take me," I said, and then I proceeded to list my arguments, one through five without stopping, so my mom could not interrupt me.

When I was done, there was a pause, and then Mom said, "All right, Grace. You may ride your bike to the Rubinsteins' house."

I couldn't believe it and threw my arms around her. "Thank you!"

My mom is more bony than cuddly, but when I hug her, she makes a low chuckling sound like doves cooing. "All right," she said after squeezing my shoulder. "Ask your father to take a look at your bicycle so we know it's safe. And I will get you water and snacks."

"I'm only going four blocks!"

"You still don't want to become dehydrated," my mom said. "And don't forget your helmet and sunglasses. How about a first aid kit?"

"Mom, you're crazy," I said. "Next you'll want me to pack a bow and arrow in case there are wild animals."

Mom nodded. "Good thinking."

It was half an hour before I was ready to leave, which was okay because the bike ride to Shoshi's is so short. In the driveway, Dad mapped the trip with his phone.

"It will take five minutes if you go via Maple Drive," he said, studying the results, "and six via Farmers Street. But Farmers Street might be better because you avoid the tricky intersection at Elm."

"I'll be fine, Dad." I stepped onto the pedal, coasted down the driveway, and swung my leg over the seat. To any ten-year-old with normal parents, a five-minute bike ride is nothing, but to the daughter of Joe Xi and Anna Burrows, it was an adventure.

"Obey all traffic laws!" my father called after me.

"Have you got everything?" My mother had come out onto the front porch.

My answer was to wave, and then I was riding away down the street on my own. It was a clear fall day and the fire-colored trees seemed to glow against the deep blue sky.

Dr. Garcia was out in his front yard raking leaves, and a big kid I didn't know was shooting baskets at the playground. Other than that, my neighborhood was quiet until, behind me, I heard a car. I didn't turn my head but stayed safely to the right until it had passed—a white SUV just like ours. . . . Wait, it *was* ours! In the driver's seat, my mother raised her hand to wave.

At the next corner, I made the right turn onto Shoshi's street. Hers was the fourth house down. I steered into the driveway, hopped off my bike, and pushed it toward the front porch. As I did, I heard a car on the street but didn't look around. If it was my mother, I didn't want to know.

The novelty of the bike ride had distracted me from its purpose—going to Shoshi's house. But now here I was, and a rush of worry filled my brain. Then, before I even had a chance to tell my brain to stop its wimpiness, I heard a dog barking as if enemy burglars were invading, and then the Rubinsteins' front door opened.

CHAPTER 15

Grace

"I don't *care* if you think I'll be cold. It's *my* body, and I'm—" The teenage girl who had opened the Rubinsteins' door was talking to someone inside and not looking where she was going until—*bump*—she ran into me and my bicycle on the porch. "Oh—sorry. Who the heck are *you*?"

Without waiting for me to answer, she looked back and called, "Shosh*i-i-i*! Some kid's here for you. Hey,

King, get back now, get *down*!" Still barking, the dog lunged toward the door—lunged toward *me*—but he couldn't get around the girl, who I guessed was Shoshi's big sister.

A woman's voice called, "Fine. *Freeze.* See if I care!"

And then the dog squeezed past the girl and jumped up with its paws on my shoulders, knocking me backward. I would have fallen, but the girl grabbed my elbow and kneed the dog out of the way. Before I knew it, the dog was back on all fours, my bike had clattered to the ground, and I had been pulled into the house.

"Shoshi! Get your butt down here!" the girl shouted, then, "Hi, I'm Molly."

"I'm Grace."

"Oh, *you're* Grace." Molly grinned. "I'm leaving. I'll stand your bike up. King won't hurt you. He's just loud. Bye."

Then she left, and I was alone in the entry hall with an enormous, panting, furry dog that had just tried to knock me down. The only dogs I've ever been around are the cattle dogs at Moonlight Ranch, and they're more interested in cows than people. Now my heart raced as I stepped away from King . . . with his pink tongue and slobbery teeth. But then he wagged his tail—that's good, right?—and trotted toward me and tried to stick his nose in a very rude place.

"Hey, no!" I pushed him away, and at the same time Shoshi appeared on the stairs.

"Leave her alone!" she yelled at the dog. Then she told me to come upstairs. On the way, she shouted, "*Mom!* Grace is here!"

So far, my main impression of Shoshi's house was that it was *loud*. Also, to be truthful, it smelled like dog.

In her room, Shoshi gestured for me to sit in her desk chair. Then she kicked a pair of gym shorts out of the way and sat on the rug.

"We'll have to share the laptop," she said.

I didn't say anything. I was too busy being amazed by Shoshi's bedroom. It was a mess! The bed was a mass of rumpled, mismatched sheets and blankets. The table beside it was piled with silver chocolate Kiss wrappers. The wastebasket overflowed. In the middle of the room was a card table heaped with crayons, markers, papers, and paint.

I had visited school friends' houses before, and they weren't all as neat as mine, but I had never been in a room like this.

Now Shoshi made her hands into a megaphone and leaned toward me. *"We'll have to share the laptop! Is that okay, Grace?"*

"Oh, uh ... sure. Sorry. Do you want to see what I've got so far?" I pulled my Walden binder out of my backpack. Shoshi grabbed papers off her desk. Then we traded.

Mrs. Keeran had told me Shoshi was a good student, and now I saw it was true. Her five facts were animals that live around Walden Pond—a fox, a field mouse, a cardinal, a red squirrel, and a black bear. Mine were stories about Henry David Thoreau and four of his friends. I had written more, but if I knew anything about the requirements at Nashoba Elementary School (and I did), hers would be good enough for an A.

I hadn't quite finished reading when Shoshi said, "I drew some pictures, too. Want to see?"

She got to her feet, and we went to look at what was on the table.

"Shoshi," I said after a minute, "those are amazing!"

"Told you I'm a good artist," she said.

Instead of regular pictures of animals standing and staring, Shoshi had painted them in action, which made each picture exciting and alive. "I should've let you do all the images," I said. "You were right."

Those words popped out because they were true, not because I wanted to say them. I hate being wrong.

Shoshi laughed. "It's okay. You were right too. I was being bossy. It's a problem I have."

"Did you get in trouble with your parents for the detention?" I asked.

"My parents didn't even say anything," she said.

"Seriously?"

Shoshi shrugged. "My sister is always in trouble, and my brother plays hockey, which my mom says is practically a full-time job for the parents. Also, they both work. I'm lucky if they remember to go to the grocery store."

"Seriously?"

Shoshi laughed. "You said that already."

"I don't have any pets," I said, "or brothers or sisters either."

"I love my pets," Shoshi said, "but you are welcome to my brother and my sister."

After that, we got back to work. She needed to add more stuff about bears, and I had more to say about Bronson Alcott, an important thinker and the father of Louisa May Alcott, who wrote *Little Women.*

We had been working only a few minutes when I heard footsteps in the hall, and then Shoshi's mom appeared in the doorway. She was tall like Shoshi with brown hair pulled back in a ponytail. She was wearing jeans and a big gray UMASS sweatshirt. There was a smudge of dirt on her cheek. Maybe she had been working in the yard?

"Shosh, I need you to help me corral Blimpy—oh!" She spotted me. "Hello, sweetie. I didn't know we had company."

Shoshi rolled her eyes. "Mo-o-om! This is Grace? I told you she was coming over? We are doing that Walden thing?"

"Right. Of course. Got it," said Shoshi's mom. Then she nodded at me. "It's a pleasure to meet you, Grace, and I'm sorry to cut this short, but we were due at the vet five minutes ago."

CHAPTER 16

Grace

Blimpy turned out to be the Rubinsteins' cat. To avoid being put in his carrier, he had scooted behind the clothes dryer and gotten stuck. Shoshi, being smaller than her mom, was supposed to squeeze back there and pull him out.

Shoshi argued that she and I had work to do, and besides, Blimpy was Molly's cat.

There was more yelling. I realized no one was actually

angry. This was just the way the family communicated. Finally, Shoshi said, "Oh, all right, but don't blame me if I flunk sixth grade."

Mrs. Rubinstein's reply was to hand her daughter gardening gloves in case Blimpy tried to fight back.

"We can meet Monday after school," Shoshi told me as she tugged on the gloves and I zipped my backpack.

"At my house," I said.

"*Now* who's bossy?" Shoshi put her hands on her hips, but she was smiling.

I rode my bike home in a very good mood. In the family room, my mother hugged me as if I had returned from jungle exploration. Then she asked me to tell her all about Shoshi's house.

I shrugged. "We did homework. Now she has to help her mom take the cat to the vet."

"Ah," said my mom, "so they have a cat as well as that big dog."

"Lots of people have pets, Mom. I would like to have a cat."

My mother shook her head. "Cats are just a lot of

fur and trouble for nothing. If you need something to cuddle, you have your stuffed animals. If you need something to talk to, you have your father and me."

I laughed. Truthfully, I was glad I was not at this moment wrestling a cat. "Hey, Mom—when you drove by before, were you checking up on me?"

"Checking up on you? Of course not. I had to go to . . . uh, the store. We were out of something."

"Out of what?"

"Milk," my mom said. "Dish soap. Oh—I almost forgot. Something came for you in the mail."

The something was a shallow box like a gift box from a fancy store, most of it plastered in silver tape. In two small squares of untaped surface area were written my address and the return address, Lucy Ambrose, Los Angeles, California, 90035.

My cookies!

I used the bread knife to cut the tape. As she watched me work, my mother cringed. "Be careful! *Please* be careful!"

Finally, I succeeded in making three long slits so I could unfold the top. "Ready?" I asked.

My mom nodded, and I lifted the flap to reveal what looked like a box full of popcorn with several sheets of paper on top. The top paper read *Please compost the popcorn* in grown-up handwriting, probably Lucy's mother's. One of the other papers looked like the cookie recipe, and there were some crayon drawings. I moved them aside and dug down to see the cookies—so many cookies!—each one wrapped in waxed paper.

"What kind are they?" my mother asked.

I pulled one out, unwrapped it, and breathed the delicious smell of chocolate chips, brown sugar, and vanilla.

"My favorite!" My mother smiled.

"Hey!" I said. "The box was addressed to *me*."

"I brought you up to be generous," said my mother.

"We'll spoil our dinner," I said.

"Not with one cookie," said my mother, "or possibly two. See? It's a good thing I went out for milk."

The cookies were delicious—just the right amount crisp and chewy. Using maximum willpower, my mother and I each ate only one before dinner and two after.

My dad doesn't like nuts, poor guy. He didn't get any.

It wasn't till later in my room that I looked at the drawings Lucy had enclosed. The first one wasn't really a drawing but more of a sign written in marker. It read: *These Cookies Are for Vanquishing the Enemy!*

The other three were crayon drawings by the three kids Lucy babysits. One, titled "Shoshi," was a black scribbled blob with red eyes and pointy claws. Arlo had signed his name to it in careful block letters.

The second, also labeled "Shoshi," showed a stick figure with pink lips and orange flames shooting out of its head. It was signed "Mia."

The third, signed "Levi," showed a tiny, many-legged bug that was about to be squashed by a pink shoe. There was an arrow to the bug labeled "Shoshi," and an arrow to the shoe labeled "Grace."

Looking at the two Shoshi monsters and the Shoshi bug gave me a funny feeling. Things had changed since I wrote to Lucy. Shoshi wasn't my friend exactly, but she didn't seem so scary anymore either.

Still, the drawings were funny, and they reminded me of Lucy. There was extra space on my bulletin board now, so I got thumbtacks out of my desk and put the three of them on display.

CHAPTER 17

Grace

In a thousand years, I never would have predicted what happened on Monday at lunchtime: Shoshi and her minions asked me to eat with them!

Before I answered, I did some quick thinking. At Nashoba Elementary, only losers buy lunch in the cafeteria, but sometimes my parents run out of time in the morning and the losers include me. Today I had a lunch from home, so that was okay, but it brought up the second question. What kind of sandwich was in it? I like tuna, but it's stinky. You couldn't eat it sitting with people you didn't know that well. Then I remembered: Today's sandwich was turkey.

"Okay," I told Nell. It was a warm day for October, so we went to eat outside at the picnic tables under the shelter. I felt funny sitting down with them. I was pretty sure other kids were looking over and whispering. *What is that runt Grace Xi doing with those other girls? She is not supposed to have any friends.*

But maybe I was imagining that. Maybe all along when I had thought people were talking behind my back, I was imagining it.

We unpacked our lunches, and the first thing I noticed was no cookies in mine. Mom must have forgotten about them. The next thing I noticed was that Shoshi had a tuna sandwich! With pickles! And nobody even pinched her nostrils to make fun of her, either.

We talked about the Walden project—Nell and Deirdre were partners. Then we talked about what we were going to be for Halloween.

"I'm too old for trick-or-treat," Nell declared. "That's for little kids."

"I'm not too old!" Deirdre said. "I'm going as a Greek goddess!"

"Seriously?" I said.

Shoshi mimicked me, "*Seriously?* That's what you always say, Grace."

"Seriously?" I repeated, and everybody laughed.

After that, things were going so well that I asked the question that had bugged me all year. "Do you guys talk every night and plan what you're going to wear?"

There was a pause, and I thought, *uh-oh, now I've done it, lunchtime exile forever.* But then Nell said, "We don't have to."

And Deirdre shrugged. "Yeah, like I wore jeans on Friday? And I'm going to wear leggings tomorrow? So I have to wear khakis today. There aren't that many choices of okay clothes to wear, you know? And after a while everybody is on the same schedule. See?"

"What are you wearing tomorrow, Grace?" Shoshi asked. "Do you want to coordinate with us?"

"Oh—I didn't ask because of that," I said truthfully.

"So"—Deirdre shrugged—"it's okay if you do."

I thought fast. "I don't think about what I'm going to wear in advance. I just grab what I grab."

This was a fib. I do plan what I'm going to wear. Tomorrow would be skinny jeans and a hoodie. But dressing the same as three other girls in my class? Even if we actually became friends? I don't know why, but the idea seemed just too strange.

If Shoshi was surprised by my clean room that afternoon, she didn't say so. What she did say was "thank you" five times to my mom for picking us up and driving us. "It sure beats walking," she added.

I didn't have piano that day, so my mom was working from home. Now I was terrified she'd say something like, "Who would allow their child to walk such a long distance?" Luckily, she just said, "You are very welcome."

The project was due Wednesday, and we didn't have that much left to finish. I moved my old stuffed animals off my armchair, and Shoshi sat at my desk, and we read over each other's writing. Because I am not a good artist, I had printed out images of each of the Walden thinkers, then put brown construction-paper frames around them. For me, that's creative, and Shoshi said it looked good.

I was adding a comma to a run-on sentence when I happened to glance up and notice Shoshi looking at my bulletin board. I looked back down at Shoshi's sentence, and then it hit me: *Oh no!*

Hopelessly, I jumped up as if I could tear down the Shoshi monsters before Shoshi live-and-in-the flesh saw them, but of course it was too late. Shoshi swiveled the desk chair to look at me, her forehead creased in puzzlement. "What are those supposed to mean?"

CHAPTER 18

Grace

I could tell my cheeks were red, and my stomach had started to churn. I forced myself to speak: "Nothing."

"Well, obviously *that's* not true," Shoshi said. "Do you think I'm a monster?"

I sighed. Lying wasn't going to get me out of this. Neither was being overly polite and apologetic. Probably, my best option was the plain old truth. "Not anymore," I said.

"But you used to," Shoshi said, and the weird part was she didn't seem that offended. Was it possible she liked herself so much she didn't need everyone else to like her?

"So who drew these?" she asked.

It was a lot to explain—Lucy, the kids she babysits, the cookies, camp—but I tried. Maybe I tried too hard. I was explaining about Hannah and f-l-o-u-r power when Shoshi interrupted: "But why did you think I was a monster?"

"Because you and Nell and Deirdre laughed at me behind my back." There. I said it.

Shoshi shrugged. "Only sometimes. And only because you acted so perfect. You even knew the number one agricultural product of Florida. Also, we thought you were stuck-up."

"I'm not!" I said.

Shoshi tilted her head to one side and looked at me. "Oh?"

"Not that stuck-up," I insisted. "And anyway, 'oranges' was the obvious answer."

Shoshi laughed. "To you. So, the most important thing I'm hearing is that somewhere in this house there are chocolate chip pecan cookies, and you are holding out on me."

"You mean you forgive me for thinking you're a monster?"

Shoshi said, "I've been called way worse than that. You met my sister, right? Now, where are those cookies? Did you say you've got some left? Is there milk?"

CHAPTER 19

Friday, December 4, Emma

Usually I empty my spam folder without even looking. But that afternoon Kayden was late meeting
me in the school library, and I didn't feel like starting my homework, so I opened it to weed junk out
and there—besides requests from all the organiza-
tions my parents belong to—was the e-mail from
Grace.

Dear Emma,

How are you?

I am busy.

Besides everything usual, my ballet school is performing *The Nutcracker*, and I play a mouse, a snowflake, and a flower. The costumes itch, especially when you get sweaty. You might not think it is possible for a snowflake and a flower to get sweaty. But it is possible. I know this personally.

At first I did not like school this year very much. Maybe you didn't know I had to skip a grade, so now I am in sixth. Things are better now. I have a friend in my class, and she has other friends who are good for eating lunch with. My good friend is named Shoshi Rubinstein. She is Jewish like you. Because of her, I know it is Hanukkah starting on

Sunday, so happy Hanukkah!

Her parents have invited me and Lily (she also takes ballet, but she is only in fifth grade) over for so+me special pancakes that you eat for dinner. As long as there is maple syrup, that is okay with me! Also we are going to play a game with a top that starts with a D. It might be called doodle. Do you know about this game?

Maybe you will be surprised when I tell you that Lucy remembered about the secret cookies, and she sent me excellent ones. Maybe it will sound even more surprising when I tell you that flour power works. I was feeling lonely, and the cookies helped me get to be friends with Shoshi Rubinstein.

!!!

So now it is your turn. Write and tell me everything! Do you have any problems? Then I will know what your cookies are supposed to do for you. Also tell me

**if you are allergic or if you hate any cookie ingredi-
ents, like sugar.**

Sincerely,

Grace Xi

**P.S. That last part was a joke. No one hates sugar.
Do they?**

Grace's e-mail brought back a flood of happy summer camp memories, all of which seemed very far away from school on a gray December day. The e-mail also made me laugh—especially the part about maple syrup and the game of "doodle." I hit reply, but just then Kayden arrived with Teacher Dustin, the librarian, and I didn't have time to write anything.

"Hey, buddy. What's the matter?" I said when I saw Kayden's frown.

Kayden's mouth stayed stubbornly closed, and I looked up at Teacher Dustin, who shrugged. "He escaped again. The head of school found him heading for the exit and brought him back."

"Kayden"—I stuck out my lower lip—"don't you like me?"

Kayden never stopped scowling. "You're okay, but I like other things better."

I said, "Like what?"

"I like video games," Kayden said. "I like cookies and TV. How come teachers get to watch TV and we don't?"

"Teachers don't watch TV at school," I said.

"Uh-*huh*," Kayden insisted. "They do in that room they got where kids aren't allowed."

I didn't know what he was talking about, but Teacher Dustin said, "Ah. You must mean the teachers' lounge, Kayden. There is a TV in there, practically an antique. I doubt it even works anymore."

"I could make it work." Kayden Haley was a second grader at the Friends Choice School in Philadelphia. I'm a fifth grader. Besides being the librarian, Teacher Dustin coordinates the Little Buddies program, where older kids like me tutor younger ones who need extra help. I've been tutoring Kayden twice a week since October. He learns fast but only when he wants to.

"We better do some dancin' before we get started then, huh?" I asked.

Kayden's frown disappeared. "Can we?"

"One song only," I said.

The dancing idea came to me one afternoon before Thanksgiving when Kayden wouldn't stop bouncing in his chair. I thought of what my parents told me about Ike, our golden retriever. When he was a puppy they had to take him for a walk or a run to settle him down. It seemed to me puppies and second graders were probably alike.

Teacher Dustin would have a cow if we danced in the library. So Kayden and I went out in the deserted hallway, and I let him pick a song on my phone, and we danced up a storm!

I am a terrible dancer, but Kayden thinks that is the best part. Watching me, he laughs and laughs—which makes me laugh too. I think he likes it that he's better at something than I am, even though I'm older and supposed to be so smart.

"Ready for some poetry?" I was out of breath.

"One more song? *Please* . . ."

"Tell you what," I said. "If you do a *fantastic* job on poetry, then we can do one more before you go home."

Kayden is supposed to be memorizing a poem to recite aloud in class. He thinks the memorizing part is easy, but every time he stands up to recite, he gets tongue-tied. That afternoon, we were still trying to find the perfect poem. We had a book by an author named Shel Silverstein. A lot of the poems were funny, and I forgot to look at the clock. It seemed like no time before Kayden's mom had come up to the library to find us.

"You said one more song!" Kayden reminded me.

"I'm sure your mom doesn't want to wait," I said.

"I don't mind," said Kayden's mom, Mrs. Haley. She is a tall, dark-skinned woman who wears her hair in braids arranged in neat rows.

Uh-oh.

Dancing in front of Kayden was one thing. But dancing in front of a *mom*?

"Well, okay then. You go ahead and pick a song and dance if you want," I said. "I'm gonna sit this one out."

"But you *have* to dance!" Kayden said as we made our way out into the hall. "Mama, you can't believe what a bad dancer Emma is. So funny-y-y-y!"

"Kayden, that's not nice," his mom said.

"Oh, no, Mrs. Haley, it's okay. He's right."

Mrs. Haley laughed. "What about if all three of us dance, then?" she said. "And I promise not to make fun."

CHAPTER 20

Emma

When my mom was pregnant with me, she read somewhere that the children of families that eat dinner together are more successful than the children of families that don't. I bet my mom has read a million articles about raising children, but that one she remembered, which is why we eat dinner as a family almost every night.

My mom is a lawyer, and my dad is the kind of doctor

you go to if you have a problem with your heart, a cardiologist. They both leave for work early in the morning, so my little brother, Benjamin, and I take turns walking Ike, and then we get our own breakfasts, put on our coats, and walk the two blocks to catch the van that takes us to school.

If we forget to walk Ike, we have to clean up the mess when we get home. If we forget our homework or our mittens, our homework doesn't get turned in or our hands are cold. Sometimes I envy kids who have a parent around to solve problems. Other times I'm proud of Benjamin and me for taking care of ourselves.

My parents usually get home around six o'clock and we eat dinner around seven. After that, they work at their desks while either Ben or I cleans up. Luckily, my parents don't cook much, so cleanup equals putting plates in the dishwasher and throwing away cardboard takeout containers.

Since it was a Friday night, the Jewish Sabbath, Mom had prepared what for us counted as a special, homemade dinner: spaghetti with sauce from a jar along with a salad from the expensive grocery store, the one where all the checkers have tattoos and even the ketchup is organic. My parents don't follow all the rules about being Jewish, but they like the rituals. So we had lit candles before dinner and said the Sabbath prayer in Hebrew.

Ike sat by my chair while we ate. When I was little, I used to drop a lot of food—more than Benjamin ever did—and even though I don't drop so much anymore, our dog stays optimistic.

When I told about tutoring Kayden, Benjamin had one question: "Did you dance in front of Mrs. Haley?" Benjamin is eight years old, a third grader.

I shrugged. "I kind of had to. She said I wasn't as bad as I thought and I should practice in front of a mirror."

Benjamin made a face. "Please promise me you'll keep your door closed. If I saw that, I might be traumatized for life." My mom gave Benjamin a warning look, but he just grinned. "I'm young," he said. "My brain's impressionable."

"Your brain is soft, you mean," I said.

Benjamin covered his head and squealed, *"Don't hurt me!"*

"Enough, you two," my father said. "Is there any other news of the day?"

"Oh yeah, I almost forgot," I said, and I told about the e-mail from Grace.

"Did someone say *cookies*?" My father perked up.

"Cookies are bad for your heart," Ben said.

"But good for your soul," said my father, which made my mom laugh. They have been married about a hundred years, but still really like each other. Sometimes it's gross.

"So if the cookies are supposed to help you solve a problem," my mom said, "what problem do you need help with?"

There was something, but I didn't want to say it right then. "Nothing much," I answered. "My life is actually going pretty smoothly."

Note to self: Do not make that kind of announcement ever again. The universe just sees it as a challenge.

CHAPTER 21

Emma

There is no such thing as a clean-your-plate club in my family because (according to my parents) clean-your-plate clubs contribute to obesity. So I was trying to decide whether the remains of my dinner—four spaghetti noodles and a dressing-soaked lettuce leaf—were worth eating when my mom asked, "Did you scan those photos for GG's book yet?"

It was the question I dreaded.

"Right," I said, which was a way to answer without actually answering. Then—leaving the last bites for the compost bin—I stood up in a hurry. It was my turn to do the dishes, and also I didn't want to be asked for details.

GG is what we call my great-grandmother, and the photos were for a book the family was putting together for her ninetieth birthday in January. My grandmother—GG's daughter and my mom's mom—was coordinating it all. Mom's and my job was to scan old photographs of GG's early life, write captions, and lay them out on pages.

Mom had thought this would be good for teaching me about family history and good for mother-daughter bonding. But she's so busy, we haven't even started yet, and it has to go to a printer by the end of next week.

Our dog, Ike, followed me into the kitchen. He is ten years old, which is old for a golden. He has a white muzzle and his eyes are cloudy. When he smells bad, my parents and I ignore it; Ben makes faces and blames me. Ike's dog bed is in the kitchen. Now he circled once and lay down.

I started loading the dishwasher, and Mom came in. "This weekend we'll work on GG's book. I promise," she said. "I just have to put in a few of hours at legal services in the morning."

Legal services is a place where people without a lot of money can go to get help from a lawyer. My mom volunteers there.

I bumped the dishwasher closed with my toe. "*And* Hanukkah starts on Sunday," I said, "*and* you have to take Ben to hockey."

Mom pushed her fingers through her hair—a gesture she makes when she's exasperated. "I know, Emma. Tomorrow night for sure. Meanwhile, you can maybe draw some ideas of how the photos will go on the pages."

"Uh-huh," I said vaguely because there was a tiny problem my mom didn't know about. I had lost the photos. Well, not really *lost*. More like I didn't happen to know their precise location at that moment.

When the dishes were done, I went up the back stairs to my bedroom. Our house is in a suburb of Philadelphia called Gladwyne, which is nice—winding quiet streets with trees on both sides, comfortable houses and big lawns. Sometimes when I tell someone I live here, they say, "Oh-h-h-h," then look me up and down in a particular way.

It took me a long time to figure out what they're thinking: *You must be rich.*

My parents would like you to know that we're not rich. We are like everyone else. Only because they both work superhard, our family has some nice things. They say we should always remember that we are lucky, and we should be generous to people who aren't.

Our house is made of stone and plaster and wood in a style called Tudor. It has a semicircular driveway in front and more rooms than we even use. When I get to the second floor, I turn right and pass Benjamin's room, then a guest room and another room across the hall.

That's the one that belonged to my brother who died.

His name was Nathan. He was five when he got a scrape on his leg that got infected, and then he got a fever. When they saw how sick he was, my parents took him to the hospital, but the medicines didn't work against his infection, and his heart stopped.

All this happened before I was born, so I never even met him. Eventually, my parents took the bed out of Nathan's room and changed the pictures on the wall. They put in chairs and a sofa and decided it was now a sitting room. But they left one thing of my brother's, his bookcase with all his books in it—*Where the Wild Things Are*, *Goodnight, Moon*, *Now We Are Six*, and lots more.

When Benjamin and I were little, my parents would read Nathan's books to us and say, "This was your brother's book, one of his favorites," or, "This was your brother's book, and he thought it was kind of boring, which is what made it good for bedtime."

Because of that, I have always known that my parents loved Nathan and that he is part of my family.

CHAPTER 22

Emma

In my bedroom, I considered my options: (1) read *The Sign of the Twisted Candles*, which was the Nancy Drew mystery I had checked out of the school library; or (2) reply to Grace's e-mail; or (3) find the envelope full of pictures.

If I did the first one first, I would feel guilty that I hadn't done the other two. And I wasn't ready to face looking for the pictures because that seemed like *work*—and hadn't I already worked a whole day at school? Not to mention I tutored Kayden?

So I sat down at my desk, opened my laptop, opened my in-box, reread Grace's note, and hit reply:

Hello, Grace—Getting your e-mail was like getting a blast of hot Arizona sunshine. (That is a simile. We are learning about them in school. Because you skipped fifth grade, you will never know about similes.)

Now all of a sudden I miss everybody so much! And I miss summer weather, too, even the sweat and the smells in the horse barn and the flies.

Do you remember the day our parents picked us up and we all said good-bye? For me, it was SO WEIRD. I never told you, but I didn't want to go to camp. It was my parents' idea. I think they thought being outside riding horses and stuff would make me less klutzy.

Ha!

At first, I was so homesick I called my parents and begged them to fly back from Philadelphia and pick me up. I even cried.

Then I got over it. Hannah would say it was because of flour power. (Hannah knows everything.)

So the weird part is by the time the day came to be picked up, I didn't want to leave camp at all.

Also, I was embarrassed about my parents.

Your parents looked so neat and tidy and full of energy, and Olivia's parents looked so handsome/ beautiful, and Lucy's mom is young and glamorous in her weird Cali kind of way. I love my parents, and they are nice (I think), but they are old for parents, and my mom refuses to dye her gray and frizzy hair, and they don't notice how they dress either, unless they are at work. (They always say they have bet-ter things to think about than clothes.) Also I think that day they actually held hands with each other. They do that sometimes IN FRONT OF EVERYONE!

Now you are tired of reading about my parents.

One more thing about Moonlight Ranch—you have to come back next year because I can't wait to see you and everybody!

There is something I have to tell you about the pancakes you are expecting at your friend's house. On behalf of all the people all over the world who celebrate Hanukkah, I apologize because there won't be maple syrup. Latkes are made of grated potato and onion. They don't go with maple syrup.

Also, the game with the top is called DREIDEL. When you play it, you win gelt, which are chocolate candies in gold wrappers that look like coins. It is a little bit babyish, but still my family plays every year.

It is so cool that you are dancing in *The Nutcracker*!
I bet you look totally cute in the costumes even if
they are itchy. My parents let me quit ballet.

You asked about a problem. I do have one, but cookies can't help.

Some pictures have disappeared. They were in an
envelope my mom handed to me, and when she did,
she said, "Put this someplace safe. It's very important. These photos are old and can't be replaced."

I am sure I did put the envelope someplace safe.

I just don't know where.

And now I can't find it.

I can't tell my mom because she is so well organized
she separates her socks by color and keeps each

color in its own special bag in her underwear drawer.
She would think this is a crisis, and I would get in
trouble, which is usually my brother Benjamin's job.

The idea of being in trouble makes me so upset, I
don't even want to look for the pictures because
what if I don't find them? What if they are really lost?

Even though cookies cannot solve my problem,
it is still okay for you to send some. I don't think I
am allergic to any of the ingredients in the recipes
Hannah gave us. Thank you for asking. Have fun at
your friend Shoshi's party!

Love from your Moonlight Ranch friend, Emma

P.S Are you going to send Vivek cookies too? You
don't have to tell :^) but one time he told me he likes
frosted ones.

I reread my e-mail and hoped Grace was patient

enough to read such a long one. Writing a lot was a good way to put off looking for the envelope.

When I tapped send, I admit that I wondered how soon I would get my cookies.

Not that cookies were the important part, of course. The important part was that Grace had remembered about the Secret Cookie Club and about camp and she had written to me. The important part was friendship.

Still, I did wonder when I would get my cookies and also what kind they would be.

It was nine thirty by now, and I was out of excuses. The pictures were in a brown envelope like every other brown envelope in the world. Even so, I was confident I would find it . . . at first.

An hour later, I wasn't so sure.

CHAPTER 23

Emma

"You've got a mystery to solve, Emma. Just like Nancy Drew." That was my friend Caitlin's assessment. It was the next morning, Saturday, after services at our temple. Along with my friend Julia, we were walking from there to the food pantry to volunteer. It wasn't that cold, but the damp was chilly, and we were all puffed up in coats, hats, and mittens.

"Car's coming—wait!" I said as we approached the crosswalk. Everyone stopped.

"I love Nancy Drew," Julia said, "especially the old ones."

"Okay, it's safe," I said, and we crossed the street.

"In the old ones, they drive around in a roadster and wear tweed skirts and cardigan sweaters," Julia said. "They never wear jeans; they wear *slacks*."

"I like wearing jeans," said Caitlin.

"But sometimes wouldn't it be nice to look nice?" Julia asked.

"I look nice if I remember to put on lip gloss," Caitlin said.

"If we dressed nice, maybe we could have roadsters," Julia said. "Maybe it all goes together."

The food pantry is where a video store used to be. One more block, turn the corner, and we were there. Because it's so close, our parents let us walk and then one of them picks us up at lunchtime.

"What is a roadster?" Caitlin asked.

"A little sports car," I said.

"A convertible?" Caitlin asked.

"I don't think so," I said.

"Well, *that's* disappointing," Caitlin said.

"Probably safer, though," I said. "Cars didn't have seat belts in those days."

"In what days?" Caitlin said.

"The 1930s—that's when the original Nancy Drew books take place," I said, "the ones written by Carolyn Keene."

Julia said, "There never was a Carolyn Keene," which was a very Julia thing to say because Julia is nice but also a know-it-all.

Caitlin said, "But her name is right on the cover."

"She still wasn't real," Julia said. "Someone just had the idea for those books and thought that name sounded right for the author. Really, they were written by different people. That's how they could get so many, and how there are still new ones now."

Inside the food pantry, the warmth felt good for about one minute. Then we got hot and were glad to hang up our coats. After that, we signed in and said hello to Mrs. Rust, who gave us our assignment: Clean up the shelves of canned goods. She didn't have to add instructions. We had done this job before.

"Got it?" she asked.

"Got it!" Caitlin, Julia, and I replied.

Our community food pantry collects food from people and stores that have extra, then distributes it to people who don't have much money. Caitlin, Julia, and I used to volunteer with our parents, but now we've been at it so long we can work on our own.

Pulling cans off shelves does not require any brain cells, so we continued our conversation.

"So how would Nancy Drew find my missing envelope?" I asked.

"*The Secret of the Missing Envelope* is not a very exciting title," Caitlin said.

"I don't care if it's exciting. It's what's missing," I said.

"*The Secret of the Stolen Photographs*," said Julia. "That's better."

"But they weren't stolen," I said. "Who would steal them?"

"Aha!" said Julia. "*Now* you're thinking like Nancy Drew! I say it was probably Benjamin, because it wasn't your mom or dad."

"Benjamin doesn't want old family photographs," I said.

"If we had all the answers, it wouldn't be a mystery," said Caitlin.

"Has anybody visited your house since your mom brought the envelope home?" Julia asked.

"Like a mysterious stranger?" Caitlin said. "A mysterious stranger would be a good suspect."

By this time our shelves were bare, so Caitlin started spraying them with cleaner and Julia wiped them down. My job was to make sure the cans weren't dented or old, then replace them on the shelves.

"No mysterious strangers have come to my house lately," I said. "But even if one did, how would I find him again to interview him?"

"It might be a 'her,'" Caitlin said.

"Finding the stranger's a problem," said Julia. "So do it last. Meanwhile, interview your parents. They might be witnesses."

"I can't interview my mom," I said. "If she finds out the envelope is missing, she'll kill me."

"You are way too unsneaky," Julia said. "All you have to do is ask questions that don't reveal what it is you're really getting at."

Caitlin nodded. "That's what Nancy Drew would do."

CHAPTER 24

Emma

Julia's mom dropped me off. When I walked in the front hall, my dad called, "Hello, Emma! How was the food pantry?"

His office is on the first floor, across the hall from my mom's. I found him sitting at the computer. He was wearing a sweatshirt with PENN QUAKERS printed across the chest in faded ink. The Quakers are the University of Pennsylvania mascot, and my dad bought the sweatshirt when he was in medical school a thousand years ago.

"We shelved soup," I said.

"That's good. That's great." He didn't take his eyes off the screen. "What's on tap for the rest of your afternoon?"

"I thought I'd break some windows and then maybe spray paint graffiti on stop signs."

Dad nodded, still looking at the screen. "Sounds good."

"Da-a-ad?"

He looked up and blinked. "Wait. What did you say? You're painting?"

"Never mind. What are you working on?"

"New study," he said. "I'm supposed to understand it by Monday."

"Where's Mom?"

Dad glanced around the office as if she might materialize.

"Still at legal services?" I reminded him.

"Oh—right. Probably. And your brother is at hockey

practice. Are you coming to his game tonight?"

"Is that kosher—hockey on the first night of Hanukkah?" I asked.

Dad shrugged. "Oh, sure. The hero of the Hanukkah story was a warrior, Judah Maccabee. He'd definitely approve of hockey."

"I'm going to keep my options open," I said. Then, with total disregard for sneakiness, I asked, "Uh, Dad? You haven't seen a brown envelope, have you?"

"What's in it?" Dad asked.

"I'd rather not say."

Dad nodded. It's pretty obvious from which parent I get absentmindedness. "I'll keep an eye out. Is it important? Life or death?"

"Yes," I said.

Dad nodded again, then looked back at the screen. "I'll let you tell your mom when you're ready," he said.

"Thanks," I said.

My bedroom is not the messiest. It's true I keep an undisturbed colony of dust bunnies under my bed, and my desk and bedside table are covered with books, magazines, papers, crayons, watercolors, glue, pens, pencils, and healthy snack foods. But I do tug the sheets up on my bed, throw my dirty clothes in the hamper, and empty my wastebasket the night before trash day.

Last year my parents let me take down prints that had been on my wall since kindergarten and tack up posters of my favorite bands and celebrities. At first, my mom thought unframed posters were a disgrace, but now she's used to it.

"It's your room," she says.

Then she sighs.

I had already looked in every drawer for the missing envelope, under every book and paper, even under the covers. Nothing. Could it be in the family room? The kitchen?

I expanded my search that afternoon. I even made Ike move so I could look under the pillow in his bed.

"You didn't take it, did you, guy?" I asked him.

He cocked his head, trying to understand.

"Nah, I know you didn't. It's the kind of thing you

would've done when you were a puppy, but now it's only worth it if it tastes good, right?"

Ike still didn't understand, but he *woofed* to be agreeable.

When Mom came home with Benjamin, I decided to follow my friends' instructions and play Nancy Drew.

"Benjamin!" I knocked on his door. "I know you're in there!"

The door swung open. My brother scowled. "What do you want?"

"Nice to see you too," I said.

"I have to rest up for the game tonight," he said.

"Are you even gonna get to play?"

My brother is one of the smaller kids on his team.

"Thanks a lot," he said—and I realized that explained his grumpy mood.

"You'll grow," I promised.

"When?" he asked.

"Not by tonight," I admitted.

"What do you want?" he repeated.

"You know that envelope of photos for GG's book?"

"No."

"Yes, you do," I insisted, and then I explained.

"You *lost* those pictures?" Benjamin said. "I can't even imagine how much trouble you're in." This idea obviously cheered him up.

"Thanks, that's helpful," I said.

"Are you coming to my game?" he asked.

"Do you want me to?"

Benjamin shrugged. "No. Yeah. I don't care."

From my brother, that was practically an enthusiastic *yes*. If he really hadn't cared, he would've plain said no.

I shrugged. "Maybe I'll go. I don't have anything better to do."

"Because you're a loser," he said.

"Yeah." I sighed. "You've got that right."

CHAPTER 25

Emma

My brother spent most of the game on the bench. Even so, his team's 2–0 win made my great-grandmother happy the next night when she, my grandmother, and two complete sets of aunts and uncles came over to celebrate Hanukkah.

GG is thin with good posture and dyed orange hair that forms a frizz halo around her face. She always wears earrings and makeup along with dresses and stockings for special occasions. Lately, she has trouble with her memory. Some people think this makes conversation tough, but Benjamin thinks it's great. Unlike the other women in my family, GG doesn't grill him for details.

"Benjamin! Such a handsome young man," she said. We were in the living room after the Hanukkah prayers were said and the candles lit. "Come here and sit by me. Now, how goes it?"

"Excellent, GG," Benjamin said. "My hockey team won our game last night."

GG clapped her hands and looked up as if God were personally responsible. "Isn't that wonderful? My grandson is a hockey star!"

After that, GG turned to me and asked about school. When I told her I got an A on an English test, she said that was wonderful too, and then she turned back to Benjamin and asked about hockey.

"It's going great," he said. "We won our first game last night two to zero!"

GG clapped her hands. "Who would have guessed?" she said. "My grandson is a hockey star!"

For dinner, we ate all the traditional Hanukkah foods—latkes that came frozen from the deli, brisket from a different deli, salad from a bag, and a lemon sponge cake my grandma had bought at a bakery. After dinner, Benjamin and I were expected to play dreidel because we are the youngest cousins and by now the only kids. All the other cousins are either in college or grown-up. I didn't mind playing dreidel too much—especially when I won a pile of Hanukkah gelt.

"Happy Hanukkah!" said the aunts and uncles as they departed. My grandmother—GG's daughter—was the last to leave, and before she did, she pulled my mom and me aside.

"How are you doing with your section of the birthday book?" she asked.

I didn't answer, and my mom said, "It will be done by Friday."

"You haven't started yet, have you?" Grandma asked.

Mom reached for Grandma and pulled her into a hug. "Nothing to worry about," Mom reassured her. "Nothing at all."

Grandma, slightly squashed in the hug, looked over my mom's shoulder at me and rolled her eyes. "If you say so, dear. Good night, Emma. I love you."

"I love you too, Grandma."

Later, when my mom came in to say good night, I almost told her about the missing photos . . . but decided against it, which is another way of saying I chickened out.

I might still find them before she ever knew they were missing, right?

Emma

Then again, I might not.

Because the next day after school, I was heading for the van to take me home as usual when I heard my mom's voice. "Emma!"

Looking over, I saw our car was in the school parking lot and my mom was waving.

"Is everything okay?" I asked as I climbed into the passenger seat. My mom never picks me up.

"Yeah, fine. I didn't mean to alarm you," Mom answered. "I just decided to take the afternoon off so we can work on GG's project."

Did you ever hear how right before you die, your whole life flashes before your eyes? I don't believe it. I have plenty of experience tripping over things, and I know as you're falling toward the ground, your brain doesn't do a single thing productive. It goes blank, which is its normal response to crisis—and this was the same as my brain's response to my mom. It did not present me with a helpful story, excuse, or explanation—it just went blank.

The blankness lasted the whole time my mom was pulling our car onto Market Street and driving toward the expressway that would take us out of the city. Finally, I couldn't stand the silence anymore. "Uh . . . we can't work on the project today, Mom," I said. "I lost the envelope with Granny's photos in it."

Imagine these words spoken in the same tones as "The Funeral March."

For several breaths after that, it was quiet.

Maybe I wasn't going to get in trouble.

Maybe my mom would understand.

Maybe pigs would fly . . . because after the quiet part, my mom turned on all her lawyer logic and let me have it.

She is not a yeller, so this was controlled yelling—yelling with the volume turned down.

My mom told me the photos were irreplaceable ("I'm sorry, Mom"), and she had taken the afternoon off work ("I'm really sorry, Mom"), and now she would have to catch up on work for nothing ("I know you're busy, Mom"), and how could I be so irresponsible? ("I didn't mean to be, Mom.") She told me she thought she could trust me ("I'm sorry to disappoint you, Mom"), and Grandma was going to be very upset ("I know, Mom"), and didn't GG deserve to have a nice ninetieth birthday? ("Yes, Mom.") She wasn't going to have another one. ("Probably not, Mom.")

My mom doesn't get mad often, and I think by this time she was almost as traumatized as me, because it got quiet again. Finally—as we were turning off the highway—I asked, "Haven't you ever lost anything?"

And she said, "No."

It takes about twenty minutes to get home from my school. Mom's rant and my groveling took only about half that time, so there were still ten minutes for where-did-you-last-have-the-envelope questions. I was still answering as best I could when we pulled into the driveway.

"I can look some more," I said. "Or we could do something different for the book, like write memories about GG or something."

Mom was still mad. "I'll think about it. First let me change my clothes."

I don't have to tell you how terrible I felt as I climbed the stairs to my room. I should have been more careful with the envelope. I should have told my mom the truth sooner. I should have looked harder. I should be an entirely different person, a well-organized person, a person who never loses anything.

Tomorrow I would become that person. I would start by . . . uh, indexing my lip gloss?

I was rummaging through the papers on my desk for the thousandth time when I heard a truck in the driveway. When I looked out the window, I saw it was FedEx.

I needed all the good-daughter points I could get, so I ran downstairs and opened the door even before the bell rang. Standing under the portico, the FedEx guy looked startled. "Emma Rosen?"

"Oh, wow. That's me." I signed, and he handed me a shallow, rectangular box.

"Have a good day."

You can probably guess what was in the box, but I was so upset my brain had turned to oatmeal, and I had no idea . . . until I saw that the return address was Xi in Groton, Massachusetts.

CHAPTER 27

Emma

"I *hate* searching for things," my mom said, "and I'm bad at it too. Never once in all my years as a kid did I find the *afikoman*."

The *afikoman* is a piece of matzo cracker that the grown-ups hide during the Passover holiday. Usually, the kid who finds it gets a prize. The *afikoman* symbolizes something or other, but really the point is to give kids something to look forward to during the boring parts of the long holiday meal.

I dunked a cookie in milk and said, "That's pathetic, Mom."

It was half an hour after FedEx delivered the box, and already Mom and I—sitting at the kitchen table— were making solid progress on the cookies. They were made from Hannah's grandpa's recipe for sugar cookies. Grace had cut them out in Hanukkah shapes—dreidel, menorah, Star of David—and frosted them in Hanukkah colors, blue and white with silver sprinkles. At first, we could hardly bring ourselves to eat them they were so pretty—but that feeling lasted only about a minute.

Mom and I knew we would have to set some cookies aside for Dad and Benjamin soon, but we weren't ready to deprive ourselves yet. Fighting had given us both an appetite.

The note in the box said the flour power was supposed to "promote good feelings between you and your mom."

Isn't that weird?

How did Grace know that would be required on the

day the cookies arrived? All I had told her was that I misplaced an envelope.

"In my defense," Mom continued, "I do have a lot of cousins. But the point is that's why I go to so much trouble to keep track of things. Because once I lose them, I will never find them."

"I get it," I said. "You're like a bat. Bats have bad eyesight so they compensate with good hearing."

Mom stopped chewing and frowned. "I'm like a *bat*?"

"Never mind. Are you still mad?"

Mom swallowed, then shrugged. "It's hard to be mad while you're eating cookies."

This gave me courage. "So, do you want to work on GG's book without the photos? We could write down some memories. It would be a start."

Mom didn't answer yes or no. Instead, she said, "What do you know about GG, anyway?"

"She was born in Europe"—I did the subtraction— "in, uh . . . 1926. And then her family came to the United States when she was around my age, around ten."

Mom nodded. "She was born in Germany. Her family

had some means and, luckily, her parents recognized how dangerous the political situation there had become. GG's father had relatives in the United States, so he and the family were able to leave and come to New York. If they hadn't, GG and the rest of her family probably would have been killed by Hitler and the Nazis."

"If that had happened, Grandma would never have been born," I said.

Mom nodded. "And then there wouldn't have been a me or a you either."

I knew about the Holocaust—when the Nazis killed millions of Jewish people and others they considered "undesirable." This wasn't only in Germany but everywhere the Nazis conquered during World War II. I had been taught about these horrible events since I was little, but they always seemed far away from my life. What my mom was telling me now made them seem very close.

"Are we done with the cookies?" Mom asked.

"For now," I said.

Mom retrieved a round tin container from a

cupboard and began putting the cookies inside. Still in perfect-daughter mode, I cleared away the milk glasses and plates and put them in the dishwasher.

"Okay," Mom said. "What if you get some paper and we'll start writing down some memories? If we have to, maybe we can use pictures from the Internet—like the town in Germany where GG was born."

"Good idea," I said sincerely, since it had been my own idea in the first place. "And maybe there will be a miracle, like the Hanukkah one when a tiny bit of lamp oil burned for eight whole days."

"You better hope so." My mom laid her arm across my shoulders. "Because if we don't find it, you're the one who's calling Grandma to tell her."

Mom and I worked on GG's book till dinnertime. Then, after dinner, Dad, Benjamin, and I looked all over the house one more time for the envelope . . . but there was no miracle.

Flour power might be strong enough to help me and Mom get over a fight, but so far it was doing nothing to solve a mystery.

CHAPTER 28

Emma

The next morning, Tuesday, Benjamin and I were putting on our coats when I had a thought. Except for being late, Kayden had worked hard, and hadn't he mentioned he liked cookies? He deserved a reward . . . besides the supreme joy of making fun of my dancing, I mean.

"Hang on," I told my brother. Then I ran to the kitchen and packed six secret cookies in my backpack for after school. Teacher Dustin wouldn't mind, provided we cleaned up the crumbs.

The school day passed slowly, with me worrying the whole time about the missing envelope. Telling my mom had been horrible. Telling my grandmother would be a nightmare.

When the bell rang at three fifteen, I went up to the library. Waiting for Kayden, I started my history homework. I didn't realize how much time had passed till I heard Teacher Dustin pick up the phone. "Do you know where Kayden is, by chance?" he asked, and I realized he must be talking to Kayden's classroom teacher. "Well, he never made it here. Yes, go ahead and call the office. We can't have small boys rampant in the hallways."

"I feel insulted," I said after Teacher Dustin hung up the phone. "Aren't I nice to him? Don't I make tutoring fun? Today I even brought cookies."

Teacher Dustin's eyes lit up. "Cookies?"

I didn't say anything. I was remembering what else Kayden liked besides cookies. "Wait a second." I stood up. "I think I know where he is."

Teacher Dustin pushed back his desk chair. "I'm coming with you. We can't afford to lose anyone else. Uh, and just out of curiosity, what kind of cookies?"

Teacher Dustin followed me down the west stairs and along the ground-floor hallway to a door marked FACULTY AND STAFF. It might as well have said KIDS KEEP OUT! and, being an obedient kind of fifth grader, I hesitated till Teacher Dustin turned the knob and pushed the door open.

At first, I didn't see anyone in the room, but the TV—big, fat, and ancient—was on and tuned to cartoons. Between it and us was a sofa. I peeked over the back and there was Kayden, immobile, goggle-eyed, and staring at the screen.

Without looking away from the screen, he said, "Told you it worked."

Teacher Dustin sighed. "I'll go to the office and tell them the fugitive's been found. You take him upstairs."

Neither Kayden nor I spoke till we got back to the library. Then he asked me, "What's a fugitive?"

"Someone who escapes," I said.

"Am I in trouble?" he asked.

"That's not my department," I said. "I just want to make sure we get something done. What does Teacher Beth want us to work on?"

"Poetry, but I *hate* poetry," he said.

"You're good at poetry," I said, "but you need more confidence about reciting."

"I feel stupid when I say those words out loud," said Kayden.

"You know when I feel stupid?" I asked him. "When I dance in front of people—like you and your mom."

Kayden thought for a second. "Huh. But you do it anyway. I guess that makes you brave, right?"

"I guess it does," I said.

Teacher Dustin came back. "Did you tell him about the cookies?"

"He doesn't deserve cookies!" I said.

"More for us, then," said Teacher Dustin.

"Did you skip lunch or something?" I asked.

"I have a sweet tooth," Teacher Dustin said.

"Cookies?" said Kayden.

"Look, Kayden, if we eat the cookies I brought, do you promise not to be late to tutoring ever, ever, ever again?" I asked.

"You brought me cookies?" Kayden said.

"I did," I said.

Solemnly, Kayden put his hand on his heart. "I promise."

I pulled the cookies out of my backpack. Teacher Dustin brought napkins and cups of milk from the library office. I set two cookies on each napkin.

Kayden frowned and poked his. "I never saw blue frosting before."

Teacher Dustin said, "They're almost too pretty to eat . . . but not quite. Did you bake them, Emma?"

"They came from my friend Grace."

Still suspicious, Kayden bit off a nibble, chewed it carefully, and announced, "Hey, they're good." After that, the only sounds were chewing, sipping, and swallowing until the cookies were gone. Then Kayden turned to me. "I have a question."

"Okay," I said.

"How did you know where I was?"

"I remembered what you told me on Friday," I said, "about how you liked to watch TV and how you thought that teachers get to watch at school."

Kayden nodded. "That was smart of you."

I thought of the missing envelope. "I guess it was if you say so. Only usually when it comes to finding things, I'm not smart at all."

"I am," Kayden said. "I have to be because I'm also good at losing things. A lot of the time, it turns up in the same place as stuff I lost before."

"You mean like one particular place?" I said.

"A couple places," Kayden said. "Either in a coat pocket, in the covers of my bed, or under my bed."

The missing envelope was too big for a coat pocket, and I had checked in the covers of my bed. "But how does stuff get under your bed?" I asked.

"I finally figured that out," Kayden said. "Sometimes when I throw junk on top, it slips down between the mattress and the wall. Under the bed is where it ends up."

CHAPTER 29

Monday, April 4, Olivia

The day of the first preseason game of the Saint Ignatius Crusaders' baseball season was *the worst day of my entire life.*

Home in my own room, I was still suffering from the trauma of what I'd been through, an hour and a half squished on cold, hard bleachers, drizzle falling on my head, goose bumps covering my body, forced to watch my star athlete brother stand around, throw the baseball, catch the baseball, hit the baseball, and stand around some more.

It wasn't one game that made my suffering so terrible; it was what I could see in my future: endless baseball torture.

I bet there are some places—like Hawaii—where the bleachers don't burn your butt or freeze it either . . . but those places are not Kansas City, Missouri, which is where my family lives. Here, the weather is usually too hot or too cold, and it is 100 percent guaranteed to be the worst possible any time a baseball game is scheduled.

If baseball is so terrible, why do I, Olivia Baron, go to my brother's games at all?

Because my parents make me!

They believe in putting family first, and if I complain, they remind me that my brother, whose name is Troy, always comes to my plays and piano recitals.

This—*obviously*—is a totally different thing, because there are a million baseball games and hardly any plays and recitals. Also, plays and recitals happen in soft seats and indoor comfort.

I have pointed this out many, many times. How do my parents respond? They cover their ears and say, "*La-la-la.*"

I am *not* kidding. I am merely *exaggerating.*

Like I said, we had been home from baseball for about half an hour, and I had escaped to my room to chill on the sofa, do homework, watch cartoons, text my friends, and play this really cute game with parakeets and pink ice cream on my phone.

That's when, all of a sudden, it happened. My iPad made the *burble-burble-ding* sound that meant I had an e-mail (*seriously? An e-mail?*), and then in its girl voice, it said, "Emma."

First I thought, *Emma? Who's Emma?*

And then I remembered.

And then I knew my day was *saved.* Moonlight Ranch! I felt like doing backflips.

But what I actually did was tuck the quilt in around me and open the message.

Hi, O. How are you? How is Kansas City? How are your parents and your brother?

Guess what? It is your turn for secret cookies.

Do you even remember secret cookies?

Mine arrived right on time from Grace (so of course they were on time). And you know what I learned? Flour power works!

I had lost something important, and my mom was mad at me. Because of the cookies, my mom got over being mad, and you could even say the cookies helped me find the lost thing. It was an envelope full of photographs, and it turned out to be hiding under my bed all the time.

(I would have looked under my bed sooner, but it's dark and scary down there, and it used to be layered with the fur of dead dust bunnies. After I got the envelope out and dusted it off and finished coughing and sneezing—then I vacuumed. My mom is still in shock.)

The photographs were for a book we made for my great-grandmother's birthday. Our family had a party, and my GG loved the party and the book, too. Her smile was so big when she saw it that losing the pictures and fighting with my mom was all worth it.

Write and tell me how your real life is going. Also, tell me what problem you need flour power to solve, and if you have any allergies or if there are any kinds of cookies you don't like or if there are any cookies you especially do like.

Love from your friend always, Emma

P.S. You have to go back to camp this summer so we can all be together again. Write and tell me that you are going! Promise?

CHAPTER 30

Olivia

I read Emma's letter twice, LOL the second time. She was still as bossy as ever!

I shoved aside the comforter, the iPad, the phone, and the remote, got up and crossed the room to my bookcase. On the bottom shelf was a photo album, and inside—*found it!*—was the Moonlight Ranch camp picture. Oh my gosh—it felt like time travel to see the four of us squinting in the bright sun. I swear,

I could feel the heat and the sweat and the dust.

I remembered how at first I hadn't liked Emma. But then she gave me the nickname "O," and that made me feel like finally I belonged in Flowerpot Cabin instead of being the rich kid—not to mention the black kid—the one everybody looked at funny. A little later, I realized Emma couldn't help being bossy. It was just who she was, but she was other things, too, like she cared about everybody so, so, so much.

"*O-LIV-i-ahhh!*" my mom called from downstairs. "*Dinner!*"

"Coming!" I called back, still looking at the picture and thinking about Flowerpot Cabin and about Vivek. There he was in the photo, looking off in the distance. Maybe he was thinking about Grace! It was so, so obvious she had a crush on him. Did he have one on her, too?

Then I wondered if I would go back this summer, and if it would be the same if I did.

"O-LIV-i-ah!" my mom called again.

"Almost there!" I stood up and went over to the

mirror above my dressing table and arranged my braids a couple of different ways. Then I squirted green apple cologne on my neck and my wrists and started downstairs.

My bedroom is on a hallway set like an indoor balcony over the foyer of our house. From it, the front staircase kind of sweeps down in a majestic curve. As I descended, I imagined there was a handsome movie star waiting at the bottom and that I was wearing diamonds and a long sparkly gown.

"How *do* you do?" I said to my pretend movie star, and then I gave him my hand, and together we spun around the shiny stone tiles.

"Olivia? What are you doing?" my mother called from the dining room.

"Dancing!" I told her.

"We're *starving* in here!" my brother called.

Oh, puh-*leez*. I spun out of the foyer, down the hallway, and into the dining room, where my parents and my brother were waiting for me. Tragically, my movie star got lost along the way.

Our house is pretty big, and it has a formal dining room, which we eat in every night—even though the table is way bigger than four people need. My parents say why would we have it if we aren't going to use it? There's a white cloth on the table and white napkins to match. In the middle there are always fresh flowers, roses from the garden in summer, pink mums from the flower shop tonight.

"What's that smell?" Troy asked when I sat down. "Did you spill a juice box?"

"At least it's better than boy smell."

"Children," said my father, "I love you both, and I have a request. Could we please get through a meal without acrimony?"

"Yes, dear Papa. Of course," I said. "Only, please could you tell me, what is this thing called acrimony?"

"Contentiousness," my mother said.

"That doesn't help," I said.

"Conflict," my brother said. "Fighting."

"Who's fighting?" I asked.

"No one, and let's keep it that way," said my mother.

"Now, who would like to give thanks?"

"I will," said my kiss-up brother. "Dear Lord, thank you for this family and thank you for this food. And please give Saint Ignatius the hitting and fielding we need to have a winning season. Amen."

"Amen," said my parents, but not me. With all the bad things God had to worry about, he might be annoyed to be asked for something as stupid as a winning baseball season—and if he was, I did *not* want to be blamed.

My family believes in table manners, so we all waited for my mother to raise her fork and take a bite of baked beans (made with Baron Barbecue Sauce, of course) before we ate.

Between bites, my mother asked about my math homework. "Did you get it turned in?"

I repeated, "Math homework?" as if the words were from an alien language.

"You forgot again, didn't you?"

I cut a piece of chicken, chewed it, and swallowed. "Mr. Driscoll didn't remind me," I said at last.

"Darling, Mr. Driscoll has two dozen other students to keep track of," my mother said. "You just have yourself."

I nodded. "I hear what you're saying, but look at it this way. It's Mr. Driscoll who cares whether I turn in my homework; therefore it's Mr. Driscoll who should remind me."

"Young lady," said my father, "you will care, too, if you get a bad grade. Engineers, scientists, computer programmers, airline pilots—they all need to do math. So do regular people if they want to get along in the world. Where would we be in our business if we didn't understand math?"

"In the toilet?" I said.

My mother made a face. "Olivia, we are at the dinner table."

"I will tell you where our business would be," said my father. "The recipes wouldn't work out, and neither would the spreadsheets. Nothing in the world of barbecue sauce works without math."

"But I'm not going to make barbecue sauce when I grow up," I said, and when I saw my parents look at each other, I added, "Not that making barbecue sauce is bad."

My father put his fork down. "It cheers me to hear you say that, Olivia, considering that you owe the clothes on your back, the food on your plate, the roof over your head, the phone in—"

My mother interrupted. "I think we get the idea, George."

"Do we?" My father looked at me.

"We do," I said. "But I am going to be . . . an *actress*."

"That's fine, but you still have to do homework," my mom said. "Does anyone want more cole slaw? I think Jenny said there's plenty."

"I do," said Troy.

Mom keeps a silver bell next to her water glass. She picked it up and rang it, and Jenny, our housekeeper, came in from the kitchen. "Let me guess," Jenny said. "Troy wants more cole slaw."

Troy grinned. "Got that right."

Jenny had the bowl in her hand and served a big spoonful.

"Thanks," Troy said. "It's delicious like always."

"It's the pineapple makes it special," Jenny said. "That's how my own mama made it."

Jenny went back to the kitchen and—unfortunately—my mom remembered what we'd been talking about. "Tonight before bed, Olivia, I will check to make sure your homework's done."

"Well, okay," I said. "I just hope I have time to finish it."

"Why wouldn't you?" my father asked.

"Because I have a very important letter to write."

"Yeah, right," said Troy.

"I do!" I explained that I had heard from Emma.

"Was she the one whose mother was wearing the shorts?" my dad asked.

"That was Lucy," I said.

"Emma's mother is a lawyer," said my mom.

"I only remember the shorts," said my dad.

My mother turned to me. "Darling, do you want to go back to Moonlight Ranch this summer? It's time to make the reservation."

"I have to think about it," I said.

"Well, don't think too long," my mother said.

After dinner, I went back up to my room. It's pretty big, I guess—bigger than the apartment my parents lived in when they were first married and trying to get the business going. Anyway, that's what they are always telling me. My colors used to be mostly pink, but after camp I decided that was too little girly, so we had it redecorated in mostly purple with red accents—like the pillows on the sofa are red, and the comforter on my bed has giant red roses. On the walls there are posters from some of my favorite movies, *The Philadelphia Story*, *Frozen*, *Titanic*, and *Cinderella*.

I reorganized myself, my remote, my iPad, and my phone on top of my quilt on my sofa. I probably would have put off answering Emma's e-mail—except I had told everyone I was going to. Anyway, it was more fun than fractions.

Dear Wonderful, Sweet, and Kindest Emma!!!

It was so TOTALLY AWESOME to get your e-mail!!!

It made me think about Flowerpot Cabin and Vivek, too, and how fun camp was!!!

Remember the last day when we all had lunch and said good-bye? I was so embarrassed about my dorky parents in their big car and how everybody looked at them because they have their pictures on bottles of barbecue sauce. Did I ever tell you how much I wish my parents made phones or computers instead of barbecue sauce?

Except I guess they could make dog food, and that would be worse, right? What if your parents had their pictures on bags of dog food? That would be a TOTAL MATTER OF MORTIFICATION.

Anyway, you asked what is going on in my life. Here is the good thing:

My class at After-School Acting Studio is putting on "The Princess and the Pea," and guess who got the part of the princess?

OLIVIA BARON!!!

(When I told my star athlete brother, he said, "I guess that's better than playing the pea.")

The only bad part is that Esmee Snyder plays the princess's archenemy the queen, which is a big part, and now I have to see her at every single rehearsal.

But I can deal with that. I can. Truly. It's not like the part of the queen is BIGGER than the part of the princess. The princess is the STAR!

As for the rest of my life—WOE IS ME!!!—it is a disaster, and not even flour-power magic can fix it.

At school, I keep forgetting to do my math homework (why do I need to understand fractions anyway?), and my teacher, Mr. Driscoll, sent a letter home saying my grade is currently a big fat F, and I am supposed to have the letter signed by my parents, but who is Mr. Driscoll even kidding? I can't do that! My parents think I'm smart. If they find out I am getting an F, my life will go down the TOILET!!!

Then there is baseball season. It is just the start, and

my brother is the shortstop, and I have to go to all his games, which RUINS MY LIFE until May at least—longer if his team makes the playoffs.

You said your brother plays hockey so you understand, right? I totally forgot you had a brother. (Sorry.) How old is he? Is he nice? He can't be, right? He is your brother.

My brother and I fight so much that sometimes I wish he would JUST DROP DEAD, and then I could be a SPOILED and HAPPY only child!!!

But he is strong and healthy, so I guess I won't be that lucky.

Now you know my problems. And you also know they are simply too ENORMOUS for flour power to solve.

On the other hand, cookies never hurt.

I do not like nuts. I do not like raisins. I do not like oatmeal. What I do like is CHOCOLATE, lots and lots of CHOCOLATE.

Now I am sending all the hugs, love, and kisses in the UNIVERSE to my very favorite Moonlight Emma—Your Most Fabulous Friend, O.

P.S. I don't know about camp this summer. It won't be the same. What if I sign up and it's not and then I am SO DISAPPOINTED???

P.P.S. Do you know if Grace sent Vivek cookies too? ;ˆ)

My mom came in before bedtime—which is nine thirty on school nights. How is a girl possibly supposed to get her homework done before nine thirty? This is still another example of how my parents are *totally* unreasonable.

"Let's take a look at that arithmetic homework," Mom said.

"Uhhhhh," I said,

"You didn't do it?"

"I don't understand it." I shrugged the giant, sad shrug of someone who really, really wished she understood the homework but—tragically—does not. "I'll ask Mr. Driscoll for help in the morning. We're allowed."

"What is it?" my mom asked. "Still fractions?"

"It's not the kind of fractions you did in school, Mama. It's a new kind. Just invented."

"Uh-*huh*," my mother said. "What if you let me see your math book? It's just distantly possible that I will remember something that helps."

I yawned and looked even sadder. "I don't think so, Mama. I'm pretty sleepy, and remember what happened last time you helped me with homework?"

My mother sighed. "I do remember."

She and I had been working on memorizing state capitals, and when I announced for the third time that the capital of California is Hollywood (it's really Sacramento), she lost it. There was yelling. There was door slamming. There was even an inappropriate word—*from my mother!*

"All right, Olivia," my mother said. "I suppose we can do it your way this one time. Do you need to go to school early, then?"

"No. Regular time. Mr. Driscoll gives us a few minutes after announcements for homework help."

Mama looked skeptical. "Since when does he do this?"

"Since, you know . . . since a lot of people are having trouble with the new kind of fractions."

My mother said, "Uh-huh," as if she didn't entirely believe me, which—since I was making it all up—did not come as a total surprise.

CHAPTER 31

Olivia

The next morning I had barely entered room 22 when Mr. Driscoll stopped me. "Olivia? Did you bring back the signed letter?"

"Which signed letter?"

"*Olivia . . .*"

"Oh! You mean the signed letter about my very, very, very unfortunate grade in math?"

"Yes, Olivia. That signed letter."

"No, Mr. Driscoll. I didn't bring it back." I smiled sadly, shook my head, and then looked humbly at my toes. "I don't know what's the matter with me. Lately, I've been forgetting a lot of stuff, and sometimes I get dizzy, too." To illustrate the point, I staggered a few steps and bumped into the wall. "It could be I have a brain tumor."

Mr. Driscoll closed his eyes and pinched the skin above his nose like he had a headache. "A brain tumor is unlikely, but if you don't feel well and want to see the nurse, you may."

I had seen the nurse once already this week and twice the week before. I had a feeling she wouldn't be sympathetic. So I squared my shoulders and stood up straight. "I feel better all of a sudden. Who knows? Perhaps I'm just a medical mystery."

By now the bell was about to ring, and most people were already at their desks. "You go ahead and take your seat, Olivia," Mr. Driscoll said. "We will talk later."

Hoping Mr. Driscoll would forget I exist, I was quieter than usual in class that day. And guess what? It worked. When the bell rang at three fifteen, I shot out the door before he had a chance to call me up to his desk.

My friend Courtney Sanchez goes to the Acting Studio too, and today it was her mom's turn to drive us to the old theater where they rent space. Inside, it was gloomy and cool, and the air smelled dusty the way it always does. Courtney and I walked up the aisle from the lobby to the stage, where the other students and our director, Mrs. Wanderling, were waiting. We did a few loosening-up exercises, and then we sat down on the floor.

"What we're going to do today is talk about our parts," said Mrs. Wanderling, also known as Mrs. W.

I don't know if you know the story of "The Princess and the Pea," but here it is, short version:

Once upon a time there was a kingdom with a prince who could not find a princess to marry. This was because of his mother, the queen. Every time a new princess showed up, the queen gave her a test to see if she was for real. So far, all the princesses had failed.

Finally a new princess arrived (me!). To test her, the queen put a single pea under the mattress on her bed. According to the queen, if the new princess was a real princess, she wouldn't be able to sleep because her delicate skin would be bruised by the tiny pea.

Lucky for the new princess, the king was on her side, and he put a boulder under the mattress. The next day the queen asked the princess how she slept, and the princess said not a wink because the bed was so lumpy.

Ta-da!

The princess passed the test and married the prince, and everyone lived happily ever after—except probably not the queen, but that part wasn't in the story.

The first character we talked about that afternoon was the queen, who would be played by Esmee.

"Why do you think the queen behaves the way she does?" Mrs. W asked.

"Because she's evil!" I said, looking at Esmee.

"Raise your hand please, Olivia," Mrs. W said. "What else?" She looked around.

Esmee raised her hand. "Because she loves her son and wants him to stay at home with her."

"*Ewww*," said Kevin, prompting a chorus of "Ewww."

Mrs. W laughed. "I think Esmee has a point. It may

be *ewww,* but it's understandable that the queen doesn't want to lose someone whom she loves."

After that, we went through every important character—the prince, the king, the jester, the wizard, even the lady-in-waiting (that's who Courtney played). At last, we got to the princess—also known as *me*! Also known as *the star*!

I had a lot to say.

"Yes, Olivia?" said Mrs. W.

"The princess is totally awesome!" I said. "She's strong and says what she thinks. She's funny. She's smart. And she's brave, too."

"That doesn't sound like much of a princess, does it?" Mrs. W said.

I was insulted. *"You take that back!"*

"Raise your hand please, Olivia," said Mrs. W. "Kevin, what do you think?"

"Princesses aren't supposed to be all that stuff Olivia just said—like strong and everything. They are supposed to be pretty and they are supposed to be nice to the prince." He shrugged. "That's about it."

"But that's so *boring*!" I said. Then I remembered and raised my hand so Mrs. W wouldn't have to remind me.

"Do you think the queen wants a strong, brave princess for her son?" Mrs. W asked.

Esmee raised her hand. "I think she wants the traditional kind, the wimpy kind. I mean *I* want that because *I* am the queen."

"But a wimpy princess isn't who the prince wants," I said. "He wants someone *cool*."

"Oh! Oh! I know." Courtney raised her hand. "Maybe the prince likes strong women because his mom is one. I mean, the queen's nasty, but she's tough, too. Maybe the princess and the queen are kind of alike."

Mrs. W nodded. "Very insightful, Courtney."

But both Esmee and I protested: *"No-o-o!"*

By this time Courtney's mom and some of the other parents had arrived to pick us up.

Mrs. W stretched and got to her feet. "Lots of good insights today," she said. "On Friday we'll start blocking, and I don't need to remind you we're off book next week. Get those lines down, everyone!"

In the car, I told Courtney her idea about the princess and queen being alike was not a good insight at all; it was ridiculous.

"Olivia," she said, "you know it's not the same as saying you-your-actual-self is like Esmee-her-actual-self, right?"

"Of course I know that," I said. "Why would you even ask?"

"Because it's how you're acting," Courtney said.

"No, I'm not."

Courtney shrugged. "Okay."

And this was even *more* irritating because I could tell she still thought she was right, only she had decided it wasn't worth it to argue.

CHAPTER 32

Olivia

"Hello-o-o!" I called when I came in the front door.

Jenny answered from the kitchen, "Hello, sweetheart!"

Jenny is usually who's home when I get back after school. For as long as I can remember, she and her husband, Ralph, have lived in an apartment downstairs in our house and helped out our family. The way my mom says it is, "Someone has to keep everything from going haywire around here while your dad and I are at work—and that's Jenny and Ralph."

Now I headed down the hall and through the dining room to the kitchen to see what Jenny was making for dinner and to snag a snack.

"Biscuits," Jenny announced as soon as I walked in. She was standing at the kitchen island rolling out snow-white dough. Behind her through the French doors I could see into the backyard. The rosebushes, trees, flower beds, and lawn all looked gray, wintry, and dead in the late-afternoon light.

I love biscuits, and we don't have them very often. I said, "Yum—how come?"

"Just a little treat for you, and besides, they go well with pork chops," Jenny said. "Your parents are on their way home, by the way."

I should have wondered why my parents were coming home early, but I was too distracted by hunger. "What is there to eat?"

"Apples right in front of you in the bowl," Jenny said.

"Will you cut one up for me?" I asked sweetly.

Jenny wiped the flour from her hands, opened a

drawer, and got out a knife. "Honestly, child, was there ever anyone so helpless?"

"Sure there was. Like Marie Antoinette, for example, and Cinderella's stepsisters. From what I hear, they were totally *useless*."

Jenny set a plate of apple in front of me. "You are funny is what you are," she said.

I looked up to say thank you and noticed frown lines between her eyes. "What's the matter?"

"Nothing, sweetheart. How was princess practice?"

I told her while I ate the apple. Then I volunteered to cut out biscuits. When my parents walked in, sixteen were lined up in neat rows on the sheet pan, and I was rerolling dough scraps.

"See what a nice job Olivia is doing with the biscuits," Jenny said before my parents could say a word.

I expected praise for being helpful, but when I looked up, I saw frowns instead—and that was when, at last, my math skills kicked in. One parent plus one parent equals Olivia is in big trouble.

CHAPTER 33

Olivia

Like you have already figured out—like I *should* have figured out—Mr. Driscoll had called my parents at work, and that's why they both came home early.

They said they were disappointed in me. They said when you came right down to it, I had been lying to them *and* lying to Mr. Driscoll. They said the lying was the worst part, worse than the bad grade in math.

If you have ever been in trouble, you know how I

felt. Partly, I was ashamed for messing up, and partly, I was angry because anger is normal if you're scolded. I thought about running away to someplace where people were nice and would understand me. I thought about throwing myself in my parents' arms the way I did when I was little and no one blamed me for anything.

Finally, my parents' anger wound down, and they got to the point, my punishment. This was it: I would have to stay after school every single day and work with a math tutor until my math grade rose at least to a B.

"But what about Acting Studio?" I whined. "We have rehearsals and—"

"Acting Studio is a privilege," my father said, "and privileges are reserved for people who deserve them. Anyway, as I understand it, your next rehearsal is on Friday, and there is a math quiz on Friday morning. Let us see how well you do on that."

"But everybody's counting on me!" I said. "I am the star!"

My father raised his eyebrows. "Perhaps the trouble is that's how you see yourself."

We were still in the kitchen. It was after six o'clock. At some point Jenny had baked the biscuits, taken them out of the oven, and gone downstairs to her apartment, but I hadn't been paying attention, not even to the delicious buttery smell of biscuits baking.

"Can I eat dinner in my room?" I asked. "Since everyone hates me."

"'*May* I?' and no, you may not, and no one hates you," my mother said.

I stomped upstairs after that, then stomped around my room a few times, too. I opened my math binder and shut it again. I would show them. I would *never* learn fractions. Not if I lived to be a hundred years old.

I heard my brother come home from baseball practice. I heard the shower in his bathroom running. Soon after that, it was time for dinner.

"Who would like to give thanks?" my mother asked when we were all seated.

I said, "I will!" which prompted suspicious looks from my parents. "It's my turn," I added politely.

"All right, Olivia," said my father.

"Dear Heavenly God on High, dear Jesus Christ, and dear, dear Holy Ghost," I began. "Thanks *eternally* for this delicious dinner we are about to receive, and thanks *especially* for the biscuits that Jenny made for me because they are a sign that at least someone around here still loves me. Amen."

No one echoed my "Amen." Instead, Troy looked up and asked, "What was that about?"

My father started to answer, "Your sister got into some—"

But I interrupted. "Don't you *dare* tell him! It's not any of his business at all!"

"Never mind," Troy said. "It's not like I care."

After that, Mom asked about baseball practice and my brother was so busy talking he didn't notice no one listened. That's the way my brother is. Totally self-centered.

CHAPTER 34

Olivia

When I walked into my class the next morning, I made myself as invisible as possible . . . but not invisible enough. In fact—I swear—Mr. Driscoll was lying in wait for me, like a tiger on the lookout for Bambi.

"Olivia? Did your parents speak to you?" he asked.

"Yes," I said.

"Then for now we'll say no more about it—except that your tutor will meet you here after school.

Please sit tight when the bell rings."

"Okay."

I swung my backpack off my shoulders, sat down, and unzipped it to pull out my binder. From her desk behind me, Sophie spoke up. "Tutor? For what? I thought you were smart."

"I am smart," I said.

"If it were me, I'd be embarrassed to have a tutor," she went on.

"Thank you," I said.

"Oh! I didn't mean you should be embarrassed. Everyone has their own unique strengths, Olivia."

Sophie is a white girl with brown hair, blue eyes, and freckles. She is not my good friend, but I never thought anything bad about her—till that moment. "Sophie?" I said. "Are you trying to make me feel worse? Or better?"

Sophie said, "Better! Obviously!"

"Okay." I nodded. "Then could you please put a lid on it?"

The rest of the day was normal except that my friends kept wanting to know why I hadn't answered their texts the night before, and I had to say about three million times, "I'm fine! I'm *totally* fine! *Really!*"

At last the three-fifteen bell rang, and I waited the way I said I would—feeling weird and embarrassed as all my friends filed out the door to freedom. The last one to leave was Sophie. In the doorway, she turned around, smiled at me, and gave me a princess wave good-bye.

I stuck my tongue out, but by then she was gone.

"Take out your math book," Mr. Driscoll said, and for one terrible moment I was afraid *he* might be my tutor. Then a girl appeared in the doorway—an eighth grader I had seen around but whose name I didn't know. She had braces and thick brown hair she had tried to tame with a headband. Standing there, she looked uncomfortable.

"Someone is here, Mr. Driscoll," I said. "Are you my tutor?"

"Hi. Yes. I am. I guess. Hi," she said.

"What's your name?" I asked.

Mr. Driscoll answered. "Olivia, this is Tara."

"We can go to the study hall," Tara said.

"That's fine," said Mr. Driscoll, "but see that you put

in the whole hour—till four thirty. Good luck, Tara."

The study hall was on the ground floor, so we descended two flights of stairs to find half a dozen pairs sitting at desks. It was like a secret tutoring society down there! Who knew?

Tara and I found a table, sat down, and arranged our books and pencils.

"How do you get to be a tutor?" I asked.

"We are supposed to work on fractions," Tara said.

"I know, but we should get to know each other first."

"Should we?" she asked. "I'm good at math, so my teacher asked me if I wanted to."

"Who's your teacher?"

She told me, and then I asked some more questions— like what she did for fun—and she answered them, and all the time I noticed the second hand of the clock on the wall spinning around, moving the Earth closer to four thirty p.m.

"Olivia, don't you have an important math quiz coming up?" Tara finally asked.

"Not till Friday," I said.

"But today's Tuesday!" Tara said. "How much do you understand about fractions anyway?"

"Practically nothing," I admitted.

Tara nodded sympathetically. "Okay. What is it you don't you get?"

I shook my head. "No offense, but that's a dumb question. If I get what I don't get, then I get it, right?"

Tara tugged at a loose strand of hair. "Let's look at chapter nine."

I shook my head no and sighed. It was a big sigh, the sigh of someone who wished very sincerely that math tutoring would last forever. "I *really* wish I could, Tara, but it's almost four thirty."

This was true. The other kids and their tutors were gathering their stuff. I had gotten through an entire tutoring session without suffering any actual tutoring!

Score: Olivia 1, Tutoring 0.

"Okay." Tara picked up her backpack. "In that case, we go back and report to Mr. Driscoll."

"Wait, what?" My heart sank. "No one told me about that part."

Upstairs, Mr. Driscoll asked to see my homework and Tara had to tell him we never got that far. Mr. Driscoll raised his eyebrows and looked at me—which wasn't fair. He *should* have looked at Tara.

"Actually, I learned a lot," I told him. "Who even knew our school had computer club?"

Mom picked me up from school that day. On the ride home, I told her about tutoring, and she said Tara sounded like an excellent role model.

"There's one thing I hadn't thought about with these after-school sessions," she went on. "You'll have to miss some of your brother's games."

I hadn't thought of that part either. *Yes!*

A few minutes later we walked into the kitchen.

"What's this?" Mom picked up a cardboard box sitting on the island. "I didn't order anything. Oh! It's addressed to you, Olivia."

"To me?" It was a second before I realized what it was.

Things were definitely looking up.

CHAPTER 35

Olivia

The secret cookies were chocolate cookies, chocolate *frosted* cookies—so many of them that my mom announced we'd either have to freeze them immediately or gain ten pounds.

"*Mom!*" I scolded. "You're not supposed to say stuff like that. The school nurse told us girls my age start to have bad body images, and worrying about our weight will only make us sick and unhappy."

Mom said the school nurse was absolutely right. At

the same time, she got plastic wrap out of the cupboard. "So we'll freeze most of the cookies to prevent breaking out in pimple constellations. Would the school nurse approve of that?"

"You're not funny, Mom. How many cookies can I have before dinner?"

"Zero," said my mom. "We will save them for dessert."

"You mean I have to *share*?"

My mother had been wrapping cookies to freeze them. Now she stopped, raised her eyebrows, and looked at me.

"I guess that's supposed to be a yes," I grumbled.

"Do you have homework?" Mom asked.

"I might."

"If you get it done now," Mom said, "you don't have to worry about it later."

"How does that make any sense?" I asked. "Worry now, worry later—same thing."

"Darling?" My mom put most of the neatly wrapped cookies into the freezer and then shut the door—with a little more force than necessary. "Math tutoring seems to have given you an attitude. Think of this as a command rather than a suggestion." She turned to face me, her hands on her hips. "Go upstairs and do your homework. *Now*."

I stiffened my arms and legs and made my face go blank—my best zombie imitation. "Must obey," I said in my deadest voice. Then, walking straight-legged, I headed for the door.

Mom called me back. I could tell she was trying not to laugh. "Hang on a second, zombie princess. There was a letter for you in the cookie box."

The envelope she handed me was fat. In my room, I dropped my backpack, kicked off my shoes, sprawled on my sofa, tore open the envelope, and tossed it toward my wastebasket.

There were three big sheets of paper! All handwritten! I swear this letter was as big as a *novel*! How could Emma possibly have that much to say?

Wednesday, April 13

Dear O,

These cookies are to help you get along better with your brother.

I know that isn't what you were expecting, and probably you think I didn't even read your e-mail at all, that I don't understand you or your troubles and that flour power can't help.

But I do, and it will.

It is important for you and your brother to get along. You don't have to agree on everything, and you can fight, but you and he are family, and you are stuck with your family in a way you are not stuck with your friends.

For example, in twenty years your brother will still be your brother, but you will have had many best friends and forgotten about them—even some of the ones you thought were BFForever. In twenty years, you might even have had more than one husband. (This happens!)

But your brother will still be your brother.

This is true even when your brother is dead . . . or you are dead.

I am saying this for a reason.

Before I or my brother Ben was born, my parents had a son named Nathan who got sick and died. I was born two years later, so all I have ever known about Nathan are his books, visits to the cemetery where he is buried, and stories my parents tell. But Nathan is still my brother.

It's true dead brothers are less annoying than live ones. I have to go to Benjamin's hockey games but never Nathan's. Nathan never leaves the lid up on the toilet seat, and he doesn't leave the sink full of toothpaste worms. Nathan doesn't make fun of my hair, and he doesn't drink a whole carton of chocolate milk that just came from the store so I don't even get one single sip. And Nathan doesn't get in trouble at school, putting my parents in a bad mood so they are grumpy with everybody for hours—even grumpy with me, who didn't do a single thing wrong.

But I would have put up with all that and put up with more, too, if I could have known Nathan for real. Maybe he would have ignored me, but I wish I had had the chance to find that out. I am a lucky person with a good life, but there is a hole in it where Nathan was supposed to be.

Here is an important thing, though. I think in a weird way Benjamin and I are closer because Nathan is gone. Because of him, we both know bad things happen and we should be grateful for each other—at the same time we are driving each other crazy.

So, anyway, that's why the cookies are supposed to help you get along with your brother.

Sorry if this doesn't make sense. Sorry if this too serious. Sorry if this letter is too long. It didn't seem right to put this stuff in an e-mail. Enjoy the cookies. No nuts!

Love from Your Moonlight Ranch BF (F?)
-Emma

P.S. Your turn to write to Lucy. She doesn't have a computer (!!!) so you will have to use snail mail.
P.P.S. See you this summer!

My grandma used a word sometimes, "gobsmacked," that means feeling so surprised it's like you've been smacked in the head. Now Grandma's word fit how I felt—gobsmacked.

Emma had never mentioned an older brother, and I couldn't imagine living with a ghost the way she did. Emma was Jewish—did Jews believe in heaven? Did she think her dead brother was looking out for her?

So far in my life, I have been protected from death and accidents and sickness—from the kind of sadness Emma's family must feel. Her letter made the world seem dangerous. If something bad happens to me, will I be tough? Or will I curl up in a ball and hide under my bed till I starve?

How do you find that out about yourself? Does something bad have to happen first?

CHAPTER 36

Olivia

Troy said grace before dinner. What he said was something stupid about staying healthy for baseball season, but because I had Emma's letter in my head I didn't say anything sarcastic; I said, "Amen."

During dinner we talked about baseball—as usual—and then about "The Princess and the Pea."

"Don't you want to play the princess in your show?" my mom asked.

"Yes! You know I do. I've almost got my part memorized."

"That's great, darling," Mom said. "But your father and I meant what we said. No B on the quiz, no play. So tomorrow you need to get serious with your tutor. Did you get your homework done before dinner?"

"What homework?"

"Olivia!" My mom shook her head. "I would hate to see you disappointed when Courtney and your other friends get to do the play and you don't."

It was quiet for a moment while we chewed, and then my mom changed the subject. I knew she was trying to be cheerful. "Olivia, do you want to tell your dad and Troy about where our dessert came from?"

Dad and Troy both echoed, "Dessert?"

I explained about secret cookies.

"They're not secret now," Troy said.

"They have secret powers," I said.

Troy waggled his fingers and made spooky, "woo-oo-oo-*oo-oo*" noises.

Usually I would have glared at him, but instead I

laughed—causing my dad to send my mom a look that meant: "How come Olivia is being so pleasant to her brother?" and my mom to reply with a tiny, supposedly invisible shrug: "No clue."

A few minutes later, Jenny cleared the dishes and brought in a plate of cookies. After one bite, we were all transported to a state of silent cookie bliss.

"May I have one more?" I asked my mom when I was done.

"If I say no, I risk the wrath of the school nurse," Mom said.

Troy looked at me, then Mom. "Are you guys speaking in code? And can I have another one too?"

"Better ask your sister," Mom said.

Normally I would've said no on principle, but I didn't. "Sure, if you want." Then I even held out the plate—causing my parents to glance at each other again.

Finally, my father picked a last cookie crumb off his plate and said, "That was delicious. But I've got desk work to do. If you'll excuse me." He stood up.

Mom pushed back her chair as well. "I've got a report to shareholders to write."

Troy and I were still finishing our second cookies, and now—*awkward!*—we were alone at the dinner table together. I figured my brother would make his escape as soon as possible, but to my surprise, he actually spoke to me. "How was math tutoring?"

"Okay," I said.

"Did you learn anything?"

"Not yet," I said.

"'Cause I had this idea about cookies and fractions. It's fractions you don't get, right?"

"Yeah," I said.

"If you let me eat one more, I'll show you."

"Ha!" I said. "Now I see why you're all of a sudden helpful."

Troy grinned. "No lie. Do you want me to show you?"

"No," I said. "You can have another cookie. But I'm the smart one and you're the athlete. If it turns out you're smart too, there's nothing left for me."

I was kind of kidding and kind of not. Troy's face said

he was listening, but then he went ahead and ignored what I had said. "I didn't get fractions at first either. What confused me was how you multiplied them and got a smaller number, but divided them and got a bigger number. It made no sense."

This was one of my problems with fractions too, but I would never admit it. "You just want to show off," I said.

My brother surprised me by looking hurt. "Suit yourself. I've got my own homework. Are you coming to the game tomorrow?"

"I have math tutoring," I said. "But what do you care? Mom and Dad will be there."

"You're right," Troy said. "I don't care. You're just my dumb little sister who can't even do fractions."

"You take that back! Just because I'm not the star athlete that everyone falls all over themselves for. You think you're so great."

Troy hesitated. "Is that what you think?"

I felt a little bad. Was it possible to hurt my brother's feelings? I never thought so before.

"Totally," I said. "I could star in a hundred shows and

Mom and Dad would never pay half the attention they do to you. And they would never tell you you can't play baseball just because you're having trouble with math homework, either. Baseball is too important."

Troy sighed. "I know, Livvy. It's awful."

Livvy is how my brother used to say Olivia when he was little. He hadn't called me that in roughly forever.

"Sports aren't even fun anymore," my brother went on. "I'm not me. I'm just Joe Athlete. And if Joe Athlete doesn't succeed—break records, get a scholarship— then he's nobody, a big fat failure. Or worse than that, just a rich kid. I don't even *like* being the center of attention," he said. Then he paused. "Not like *some* people."

I might've been mad about that last part, but I was too surprised. "I didn't know—" I started to say, but my brother kept talking.

"Here's the thing, Livvy. I'm sore all the time. People think football is tough, but our coach works us like crazy. Sometimes after practice I'm so tired I think I'm going to die."

It is too bad my brother had to go and say all that, because on top of the letter from Emma, it made something happen in my head that I totally didn't expect . . . and neither did Troy.

"*Don't die!*" I wailed, and then I started to cry.

Poor Troy. His eyes were big as saucers. "Holy rats, Livvy! I didn't mean it for reals! Sheesh—" He handed me a napkin. "I knew you were a drama queen, but this is ridiculous."

I sniffed back tears and told him about the letter from Emma. This time he listened.

"Awww," Troy said when I was done. "That's tough for your friend, but that kid's not me, and most people's brothers grow up, you know. I'm going to grow up too."

"I hope so."

"And another thing," said Troy. "You don't need a tutor. I can help you with fractions. Only it's hard for me to find the time with practice and everything."

"Do you really hate it?" I asked. "You could quit. You could explain to Mom and Dad . . ."

Troy shook his head. "No, I can't. People are

counting on me. Maybe after the season's over."

"Thanks for offering to help with fractions," I said.

"Can I make another suggestion?" Troy asked.

"If you have to."

"Take your tutor some cookies."

CHAPTER 37

Thursday, May 19, Lucy

I must have been facing the wrong way when the soccer ball hit me in the head. All I know for sure is one second I was standing on the field at school waiting for the whistle to blow, and the next I was lying flat on the grass, looking up into the pale gray sky. My right ear was stinging.

Then the worried faces gathered around.

"Lucy, how many fingers am I holding up?"

"Who's the president? What day is it? Do you know the year?"

"On a scale of one to ten, Lucy, how much does it hurt?"

I couldn't think about so many questions at once. So I didn't answer, just blinked a couple of times . . . and then the faces seemed even more worried.

"We'd better call nine one one," said Mrs. Kamae, my PE teacher. "We can't take chances with concussion."

"Wait—no, Mrs. Kamae," said my best friend, Emmaline Woolsey. "I think it's just Lucy being how she always is. Are you okay, Lu?"

I sat up and rubbed my ear. "Fine, I think."

"No stars? No headache?" Mrs. Kamae asked.

"Stars?" I was confused.

"I *mean*," said Mrs. Kamae, "you don't see stars flashing in front of your eyes?"

"It's daytime, Mrs. Kamae," I said.

Emmaline looked at Mrs. Kamae. "See?"

Mrs. Kamae nodded. "Yeah, she's fine. But to be on the safe side, Lucy, I think you'd better sit out today."

"No!" I protested. "My team needs me!"

It was true, too. I'm not usually good at games. I don't have what Mrs. Kamae calls "killer instinct." (She had to explain she didn't mean that literally. She just meant I'm not very aggressive.) But for some reason, when I kick a soccer ball, it goes where I aim it. I have a "knack," Mrs. Kamae says. She wants me to go out for the school team next year.

"You can play tomorrow," Mrs. Kamae said. "And tell your mom if you feel funny later—nauseated, or anything."

"I will," I said, not bothering to explain that I might not even see my mom later. She had a new waitressing job, and if she went out after, she often didn't get home till I was asleep. I could tell my grandmother, maybe, but she'd just tell me to drink a cup of tea, and could I fix one for her while I was at it.

School ends at three fifteen. Clarissa's mom gave me a ride home, as usual. Clarissa and I are the only kids in my neighborhood who go to public school—me because we don't have the money for private and Clarissa because her dad is on the school board and it would look bad if he sent his daughter to private school. Clarissa's mom is always nice, but I feel like a mooch for getting rides all the time.

Some days I walk, but on Thursdays I can't be late for my job watching Arlo, Mia, and Levi.

Inside our house it was so still it felt like no one had moved since morning when I left. "Hello Nana!" I called. She didn't answer, but I didn't worry. She is a little deaf and spends most of the time in her bedroom, which is on the far side of the kitchen.

I dumped my backpack on my bed and looked around for something to wear to watch the triplets.

My room used to be as gloomy as the rest of the house, but last year I asked my mom if we couldn't do something about it, and to my surprise she said why not? So we went to a paint store and spent a whole weekend turning the walls bright yellow.

Then I made collages out of old magazines and comic books and whatever I could find and sprayed them with lacquer and hung them up. So now, even if the bedspread is ancient and the dresser wobbles and sometimes my clothes are mounded on the floor in a heap, at least my room is colorful.

Now I kicked off my shoes and traded my capris

for gym shorts and my top for a ratty old T-shirt of Mom's. It's not like my school clothes are so special, but babysitting usually equals grass, jelly, and juice stains, and laundry is not my favorite chore.

Clothes changed, I made my way through the house to check in with my grandmother.

"There you are, Nana. Have you even been out of your bedroom today?" I asked.

My grandmother has long streaky gray hair that she pulls back and then clips on top of her head in a free-form sculpture that's different every day. She wears Levi's and T-shirts with the names of old bands on them—the Grateful Dead, the Beatles, Jefferson Airplane. She almost never wears shoes because she almost never goes outside. Her skin is pale as paper.

Now she was sitting in the room's only chair, reading a fat book. The blinds were drawn and a lamp was on.

"No reason to go anywhere," Nana said. "I've got everything I need right here."

"It's Thursday, so I've got babysitting, remember?" I said.

"Lucy, I am not demented. I *know* the days of the week."

I ignored this and nodded at the book in her lap. "Which one is that?"

"*Bleak House*," she said.

My grandmother only reads books by Charles Dickens. "Is that the one with Jarndyce versus Jarndyce—the legal case that never ends?"

Nana nodded. "I like the depiction of evil lawyers futilely beavering away at meaningless work. It's like the real world, only it's funnier."

My grandmother believes lawyers cheated her out of her money, leaving her—and my mom and me—in "straitened circumstances," aka broke. Also, my grandfather was a lawyer, and he and my grandmother got divorced when my mother was little, long before I showed up on the scene.

"I have to go," I said.

"Give Maya, Rambo, and Leland my regards," Nana said.

My grandmother knows the triplets' actual names perfectly well. It's no use trying to correct her.

"Yes, ma'am. I will. See you for dinner."

We live in a town that's known for being wealthy—Beverly Hills—and our house is the smallest and most ordinary on our street, maybe in the whole town. It was built in the 1940s in a style called "ranch," which has nothing to do with the salad dressing or with horses and cows. It just means it has only one floor. Most of the other houses on our street are new enough that I remember when they were built. One by one, little ones like ours were torn down and gigantic ones went up. Now our house looks like a midget among giants.

Anyway, with the low ceilings and the drapes closed, our house is kind of dark, which my mom says is just as well because it makes it harder to see the peeling wallpaper, dust, and shredded places in the furniture where Mitzi the cat (she's dead now) sharpened her claws. Because its floor is black slate, the front hall is even darker than the other rooms. This explains why I didn't notice till now—when I was almost out the door—that there was a letter on the hall table addressed to Lucy Ambrose.

My mother must have gotten the mail today on her way to work and then come back and set it there for me.

I thought it was from my dad until I picked it up and saw how nice the paper was—cream-colored stationery, not like a greeting card you'd buy at Thrifty Drug. Also, my name and address were printed in type. There was no return address on the front, but when I flipped the envelope over, I saw an address on the flap in slightly raised letters—Kansas City, Missouri.

Oh. My. Gosh.

Olivia!

For a minute I couldn't believe it. Secret cookies had really happened! Way back last summer we had planned it, and way back last fall I had sent cookies to Grace. Then Grace had sent cookies to Emma and Emma to Olivia—and I was the last link in the chain. It had come full circle just the way it was supposed to.

What were the odds of *that*?

CHAPTER 38

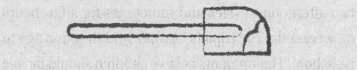

Lucy

I wanted to read my letter, but I couldn't be late. So I laid it back down, flew out the door, and ran.

The triplets live at the end of the cul-de-sac in one of the big new houses. Because of the way the dead end is arranged, they have the biggest backyard on the street. Kendall, their mom, says this is a blessing because the triplets can run around and yell without bothering anyone on the patio or in the house. But it's a curse because they are easy to lose track of.

Since last fall, I have had the job of watching them two afternoons a week and sometimes for a few hours on weekends. The triplets are four, and they don't go to preschool. Their parents believe children should be free to explore the world around them in an unstructured free-form play-focused manner until they are ready for kindergarten. I think Kendall read some book about this when she was pregnant. Arlo, Levi, and Mia don't even have to wear clothes unless they want to, and I am not allowed to discipline them, only to "point out the consequences of poor choices."

Nana says the three of them sound like little savages; Mom says they sound charming. I think they're somewhere on the overlap between.

When I arrived that day, Kendall was standing by the window next to the front door, waiting. The kids ran in circles around her like excited poodles.

Arlo and Mia shouted, "Lucy!"

Levi shouted, "Woo-see!"

Kendall exhaled a big sigh. "Thank goodness you're here."

"How is everybody?" I asked, happy to see them—even though Levi had a snot mustache, the spaces between Arlo's toes were caked with mud, and Mia's hair was still recovering from the haircut Levi gave her last week with craft scissors.

(Kendall told me she looked away for only *one second* to answer a text, and—*snip*—Mia had a bald spot.)

Even so, they were adorable and they were happy. And since it was me being there that made them happy, how could I not be happy back?

"Anything I should know?" I asked Kendall as we made our way to the kitchen. Forward progress was slow because three children were tangled around my legs.

Kendall told me the news of the triplets' day—food spilled, games abandoned, damage inflicted, books read.

"Wow, you must be exhausted," I said.

"Oh, I am," Kendall agreed. "In fact, I was hoping to

take a little catnap while you watch them. Of course, I'll be right here if you need me."

Last fall, when I started watching the triplets, things didn't always go so smoothly. The way the kids saw it, my job was to keep their mom from them, which made their job bothering her as much as possible. If Arlo couldn't find his favorite book, or Mia fell down, or Levi wanted a snack, they went to her and complained. I felt like I was getting paid for nothing.

I don't know when exactly things changed, but they did. Maybe I got the hang of watching them. Maybe they started to trust me.

Anyway, I have to say I've learned stuff about kids since fall, and now Kendall says she couldn't get along without me.

"Hungry?" I asked them.

It was a rhetorical question, which means one where you know the answer already: Of course they were hungry!

But here is an example of what I've learned: Never ask little kids what they want to eat. If you do, they will place an order, change their minds, and place a new order . . . and what you'll do all afternoon is make snacks. So instead I set the menu myself. That day it was ants on a log (celery with peanut butter and raisins), sliced apples, baby carrots, and goldfish crackers—all organic, non-GMO, and fair trade, of course.

At my own house, no grown-up ever thinks to buy snacks, so I fixed myself some too, and then the four of us ate on the patio.

After that it was playtime. Sometimes we wrestle, sometimes we read books, sometimes we play pretend, and sometimes we paint. That day it was soccer. The triplets have a green half-size ball and little plastic soccer goals that we get out of the garden shed and set up at either end of the yard. We played three-on-one— triplets against me. The boys play tackle soccer, their own invention. Mia cheats and uses her hands.

There are plenty of arguments and sometimes tears, but not so many freak-outs anymore. As long as there's laughing—and all the owies can be fixed with Band-Aids—I figure we are doing okay.

We were outdoors all afternoon and so busy that

when Kendall—looking calm—came out to tell us it
was six o'clock, I was surprised.

"Watch me kick, Mommy!" Mia said.

"No, watch me!" Arlo insisted.

Levi just grinned.

"Magnificent!" their mom told them. "Would you like
to stay for dinner, Lucy?"

"*Stay! Stay! Stay!*" Mia and Levi grabbed my legs while
Arlo clung to my right arm.

"Wait . . . dinner?" I said. Sometimes it takes me a second to make my brain move from one idea to another.
Right then it had been busy thinking about how the
triplets are getting better at soccer. I hadn't been thinking of dinner at all. But no, I couldn't stay for dinner.
Somebody had to make something for Nana. Otherwise
she would try to live on nothing but sugar-free yogurt.

"I can't," I said. "I'm sorry. Thanks for asking."

I didn't think of O's letter until I was walking home.
Even so, I didn't have a chance to read it right away.

The second I opened our front door, Nana called,
"What time is dinner?"

She was in her room but still must have heard me come in. I have noticed when she wants something her hearing improves.

"I'm home, Nana," I called. "I'll get right on it."

In the kitchen, I boiled whole wheat noodles and tossed them with butter, nuked frozen broccoli and a can of garbanzo beans (drained).

I moved a stack of mail out of the way so that Nana and I could sit at the kitchen counter to eat. She asked about school and then about the health of "Warren, Maria, and Larry." I'm not sure she paid attention to my answers. I would have asked about her day, too, but I already know the plot of *Bleak House*.

After dinner, I washed up. My mom or my grandma would have done it eventually, but I learned from triplet duty that dirty dishes are harder to wash if they sit around; the food dries on them, and you have to scrub. It's better just to get it over with.

And besides, you can think while you wash the dishes. I was thinking about my bricolage for art class. A bricolage is a sculpture made from whatever you find lying around—sort of like a collage in 3-D. Mrs. Coatrak, the art teacher, thinks I'm some kind of star student, and Monday she told me she might enter mine in a citywide contest.

I said, "Okay, Mrs. Coatrak. Only I don't know what it is yet."

"Let your ideas *flow*!" said Mrs. Coatrak. "Trust the process!"

If you don't know what she was talking about, that makes two of us, but my mom was an art major in college, and sometimes she talks about art and creativity the same way. My mom was a good painter, I guess. A long time ago, some of her watercolors were even in fancy galleries. I remember she used to paint when I was little—when my dad still lived with us—but she hasn't painted in a long time.

As for my project, so far I had bent a fat cardboard strip into the shape of a heart, like a frame.

But what was my heart supposed to mean, anyway?

Since I was in the kitchen, I started to think about hearts and kitchens. And after I put the dishes away, I unpeeled the label from the bottle of dish detergent.

Then I went in the recycling closet and pulled out empty boxes of granola and pasta, the label from the package of frozen broccoli, and two yogurt containers.

I still had no idea what I was doing, but this was a start.

I saved O's letter for my treat after homework. It was almost nine o'clock when at last I opened the envelope—which was lined with red foil—and read:

Saturday, May 14

Dearest Darling Most Special and Exalted Lucy,

Excuse me, but this is REALLY, REALLY, REALLY weird.

I am typing a letter that I am going to PRINT OUT and put in an ENVELOPE and MAIL!!! Before I mail it, I am going to have to ask a grown-up to show me how to write an address on an envelope because I can never remember the right way.

Now, Lucy. I must tell you something like I was Hannah or some other big-sister person. I remember sometimes how you are an artist who likes to think about big, important things rather than small ones like where you are stepping (into a cow plop—remember that time?) or what you did with your toothbrush (under your pillow—why did you put it there?), but NOW it is important to FOCUS. You must ask your mom something. You must ask her to buy you a computer and a phone. Otherwise, you cannot communicate with your friends and be a REGULAR PERSON!!!

Can you please remember to do that? Maybe you can write it down right now someplace you will see it, like in ink on your arm!!!

Here is another important thing: HOW ARE YOU?

I am REALLY, REALLY, REALLY fine!

Let me tell you about my life. Last weekend I got to

play the part of "princess" in "The Princess and the Pea," and everybody says I was excellent.

I am sorry if that sounds braggy, but I also don't care. I worked hard to memorize my lines and then to get everything about the part just right. Some people say I was already good at being a princess (like my brother, who thinks he is TERRIBLY FUNNY), but the truth is you have to work hard to be an actress, and I did, and it was TOTALLY worth it.

To play the part I also had to learn math!!!

I know that sounds weird.

I was FLUNKING math and I had to get a tutor and she helped me learn to do fractions, and here is where flour power comes in. You will never believe it—but it really works! Just like Hannah and her dead grandpa said.

Anyway, Emma (it was her turn) sent me cookies, and I

took cookies to my tutor, and she cut them up to show me how if you have a half of a half it equals a quarter, and all of a sudden multiplying fractions made sense!!!

Then we got to eat the cookies.

Against ALL ODDS, it was my brother who had the idea of taking cookies to my tutor, which is not only amazing that he would have a good idea but also that I actually listened to him because we didn't even like each other, which was partly because I was jealous because he is a star at baseball and my parents go TOTALLY CRAZY for baseball.

But then we had this talk while we ate Emma's chocolate cookies, and now we understand each other better.

My brother even helped me practice my lines for the play, so to be fair I offered to practice baseball with him, too, but he said that was unnecessary.

So now you have to tell me all about your life!!!

Is there anything in it that is not perfect? Because the secret cookies will help—you can trust me on this.

Are you going back to Moonlight Ranch this summer? Emma (you know how bossy she is) told me I have to! And I kind of want to because I miss you guys. But I'm scared that we won't be in the same cabin again, and then I'll be disappointed, and I HATE being disappointed. Anyway, if you don't go to camp and I do then I'll DEFINITELY be disappointed. So tell me what you're going to do.

I am REALLY, REALLY, REALLY looking forward to getting your letter!!!

Love, Your Favorite Princess (JK) from Flowerpot Cabin—O

P.S. What kind of cookies do you like? And don't say

barbecue sauce cookies!!! People think jokes like that are funny, but not if you're me.

I put the letter back in its envelope and laid it on my desk. I got ready for bed. I went back to Nana's room to say good night and—surprise—she was in her chair reading. I didn't tell her about the letter. She might have been interested, but I was feeling bratty, wanting to hold on to something for myself.

It wasn't till I climbed into bed and turned out the light that I thought about what Olivia had written.

It was cool that flour power had worked for O, for Emma, and for Grace.

But their problems were nothing like mine. They probably had clean houses with stoves where all four burners worked and refrigerators packed with food (even snacks and ice cream).

At Moonlight Ranch the differences between me and them were not so obvious. But I bet none of them would be able to imagine a real-world life like mine, not even for a single minute.

Then I thought about Moonlight Ranch—and realized I really (REALLY, REALLY!!!) wanted to go back, but
I had no idea if I'd be able to. My aunt Freda in Santa
Barbara had paid last summer. She is my dad's step-
sister, who somehow manages to get along with my
mom and my grandma still. So far this year she hadn't
said anything about it.

I must have just fallen asleep when I heard knocking
on my door. "Come in, Mom."

"Did I wake you?" Her voice was soft.

"I'm okay. How are you?"

Mom sat down on the edge of my bed. "My feet hurt."

"How were your tips?"

"Meh." She shrugged. "They won't change our life-
style. Oh, say—what was that letter all about? At first I
thought it was from your father. I was kind of hoping he
might've sent a check—but then I saw the Kansas City
postmark. Is it from one of your camp friends?"

"It's from O—from Olivia," I said.

"Ah, the barbecue sauce heiress," Mom said.

"She hates when people say things like that," I said.

"Then I won't, at least not in front of her," Mom said. "How is Olivia?"

I told her, and how the cookies would be coming, too—just as soon as I wrote back. Mom said, "I'm impressed with all four of you. It's not easy to maintain camp friendships during the year. Do you want to go back to Moonlight Ranch this summer?"

You already know the answer to that one, but I knew it was hard on my mom that she couldn't give me things, so I tried to sound casual. "Yeah, I guess. I had a good time."

Mom sighed and said, "We'll see." Then she gave me a squeeze and a kiss. "Good night, honey."

CHAPTER 39

Lucy

The next day at school was completely ordinary except that we had art, which is only twice a week. You already know about my bricolage. That day, I cut out pieces of the labels, the mail, and the recycling that I'd brought from home. Some I glued to my cardboard frame, and some I suspended inside the frame from clear thread. Then I painted some numbers and suspended them, too. They were supposed to look like the ones on the microwave timer.

Emmaline was working beside me. Her bricolage was made of old coat hangers twisted into a shape like a birdcage. She had been trying to decide what to put inside.

Mrs. Coatrak stopped by and watched us work. "Wonderful! Wonderful! So creative," she said. "Never mind the structural issues, Lucy. Those we can work out later."

"Structural issues?" I repeated. "Are there structural issues?"

"You know," said Mrs. Coatrak. "Like how will you get it to stand up? It isn't going to balance very well on its point."

"It isn't?" I said.

"*Duh*, Lucy," said Emmaline.

"Oh," I said. "I hadn't thought of that."

I don't watch the triplets on Friday, and I had all weekend for homework. So after I got home and greeted

Nana and made sure there was something to scrounge for dinner, I got out pen, stationery, and the letter from O to write her back.

Friday, May 20

Dear Equally Exalted and About-to-Be World Famous O,

It was awesome to get your letter and to think about Moonlight Ranch and you and Emma and Grace (and Hannah and Vivek). I forgot I missed you till your letter arrived.

I am fine too, because-like Nana would say-I am healthy and young. It is wrong to complain, she says, when you have food to eat and a roof over your head and not even a cold or a headache.

Even after my cat died, I did not complain. She was only a stray cat

anyway. Easy come, easy go, Nana said. I
buried her in the weeds that used to be
a flower bed. My mom felt bad too, and
she and I stood over the grave, and she
read a poem about cat names by Eliot-
somebody. Then I cleared the patch of
weeds and put up a rock-and-Popsicle-
stick headstone and planted marigolds,
so now there is a tiny square in our
yard that looks loved.

    Change of topic: I have to explain
something and I hope you will not think I
am being pathetic. I would really, really,
really (!!!) like to go back to Moonlight
Ranch this summer.

    We must all obey Emma, right?

    But also I liked being there. Even
though Grace and Emma and you and I
were all different, we were all the same
because we did cleanup chores together
and lived in Flowerpot together and ate

together and practiced for the talent
show together.

Does that make sense?

Change of topic: I know how you want
me to get a phone or a computer, but
this is impossible because my nana does
not believe in screens. She thinks they
are bad for developing brains, and she
thinks my brain is still developing.

A standing ovation from me for your
super job playing the princess! Way to
go, O! At school, I am working on an art
project that my teacher says she is
going to submit for a prize if I can keep
it from falling on the floor and getting
destroyed. I like making art like you
like theater.

I guess I want flour power to help me
figure out a way to go to Moonlight Ranch
this summer, but I don't see how that's
possible. I like most cookies, I think. I

will probably share with Arlo, Mia, and Levi, and it will be easier if I don't have to clean them up after, so maybe not messy cookies.

Love ya always, Lucy

P.S. Did you see on the last day of camp that Vivek gave Grace something? And I asked Grace about it, too, but she won't say what!

I didn't have a cookie sticker, but I had some glittery cupcake ones that had been party favors at Emmaline Woolsey's birthday, so I put two on the envelope, and then I stamped hearts and ponies on it with my green inkpad, the only one that wasn't dried up.

The next afternoon, Saturday, I was supposed to watch the triplets for a couple of hours. On the way down the street, I noticed a missing cat flyer posted on a stick in the front yard of one of our neighbors: REWARD! MUCH BELOVED PET MISSING. PLEASE CALL BRIANNA, and the phone number.

At Kendall's house, the triplets attached themselves to my arms and legs while I told their mom about the flyer.

She shook her head. "Poor Brianna. On the news they're saying predators like raccoons and coyotes are extra bold this year because it's been so dry. They get thirsty and hungry, too, so they come into neighborhoods like ours and scout around."

"You mean they scout around for *pets*?" I said.

Kendall shrugged. "If they find them—and also pet food if you leave it outside, and trash, and water from the garden hose. Poor things. They're just trying to live too."

The next week I scored four soccer goals in gym class the next week, and in art I worked on my bricolage. Finally, on Friday, I solved the "structural problem" by hanging the whole thing from the ceiling like a mobile.

"Wonderful! Beautiful!" Mrs. Coatrak said.

"Does it have a name?" Emmaline asked me.

"It does," I said. "'The Kitchen Is the Heart of the Home.'"

Emmaline frowned. "What's that supposed to mean?"

I shrugged. "I thought of it while I was doing dishes. Maybe because it's where families eat? So the only time they're ever together is in the kitchen. And, you know—love? Togetherness? Family?"

"You don't even like your family," Emmaline said. "You always say your mom tries to act your sister, and your grandma is mean."

"Do I?"

"*Yes,*" said Emmaline.

"I don't mean it," I said.

"Then why do you say it?"

"I mean it when I say it but not the rest of the time," I clarified.

Our family history is kind of different. My dad is a lot older than my mom. She quit college to marry him when he had a big job and a lot of money, but then he did something wrong, something called fraud, which is a kind of stealing. He had to go to prison; there wasn't any more money; my mom and I moved in with my grandmother.

I was in kindergarten when my dad got out of prison. I thought things would be like before, but my mom didn't want to be married anymore—or anyway, not to him. So they got divorced.

Now sometimes he sends me funny cards.

"It's a good thing I'm your best friend," said Emmaline, "because otherwise I would think you're really weird."

"I know it's good," I said, and then I looked at Emmaline's project. "Change of topic: What are you going to put inside your birdcage?"

In the art room, we sit on tall stools to work. Emmaline's backpack was under her stool. Now she reached down, unzipped a compartment, pulled out a Lego piece, and showed me.

"Is that Princess Leia?" I asked.

"I'm going to glue her to a cork from a wine bottle, like a pedestal. Then glue the whole thing in the middle of the cage," she said.

I thought for a minute. "So is it about how freedom suffered in the time of the empire—in the Star Wars movies, I mean?"

"Yeah, that's it," she said. "And also she was the only Lego piece my little brother would let me borrow."

I laughed. "And you're saying *mine* doesn't make sense?"

"Mine doesn't have to. *You're* the artist," Emmaline said.

I looked back at my heart. "It still needs something."

That night in the kitchen, I was moving the mail aside when I saw an envelope with the return address of Moonlight Ranch and red letters: LAST CHANCE.

Uh oh. Would Aunt Freda come through? Had she gotten the same letter?

CHAPTER 40

Lucy

In my house, phone calls don't usually last longer than a grunted "No thanks" and the click of Mom or Nana hanging up. But when the phone rang the next morning, I heard Mom's singsong voice from the living room and knew she must be talking to a real person.

Maybe Aunt Freda? And if so, was she telling Mom she could pay for Moonlight Ranch again this year? I crossed my fingers.

The singsong continued and then got louder, to the point where I could understand what my mother was saying: "She's right here in her room, Freda, no doubt doing homework. You know how conscientious she is. Hold on."

My mother knocked, and I counted to ten before opening the door. My mom mouthed, "Aunt Freda," then rolled her eyes and opened and closed her hand in the sign that meant "yak, yak, yak."

I took the phone from her. "Hello, Aunt Freda. How are you?"

"Lucy! How nice to hear your voice. How have you been? Tell me what's new at school. Tell me everything."

I told her about the triplets and school and my bricolage, and she listened. As far as I could tell, she wasn't driving or cleaning the bathtub or shaving her legs either. She was giving me all her attention.

"Fantastic!" she interjected at appropriate moments, or, "Oh dear. That's not optimal."

Finally, I realized I was going yak, yak, yak. "Oh, Aunt Freda, I'm sorry," I said. "You probably have other things to do."

"Nothing more important than you, Lucy. I am so glad to hear all your news. Now, listen, I have something to tell you, too, and I hope it won't be devastating."

My heart sank . . . and so did I, right down onto my bed.

"Honey, I've had an unfortunate year in the finance department, and I just can't see my way clear to pay for Moonlight Ranch this summer."

To keep my voice steady, I paused before I answered. "That's okay, Aunt Freda. I might be too old for summer camp anyway."

"Oh?"

"I really liked it last year," I reassured her. "Thank you again for sending me."

We didn't talk much longer, and when I said good-bye I took the phone back to the living room and dropped down on the sofa. I told my brain not to think about Moonlight Ranch or Flowerpot Cabin or Grace and Emma and Olivia—so what my brain did was think about Moonlight Ranch and Flowerpot Cabin and Grace and Emma and Olivia.

Typical.

It didn't make me feel better that the sunlight filtering through the frayed old drapes revealed how dusty and shabby the room was.

It doesn't matter, I told myself. We only use the living room as a hallway. No one ever visits us, and when my mom and Nana and I are home at the same time, we hide out in our own bedrooms.

I don't know how long I sat there, but finally the *whoosh* of brakes outside told me a truck had stopped. The mail? No, it was too late for that. I turned around and looked out—a FedEx truck. That was unusual. We never order anything . . . and now the driver was coming up the walk carrying a box.

Probably a mistake.

I went to the front door and opened it at the same time the driver rang the bell.

"Lucy Ambrose?" he asked.

"Oh, that's me," I took the box.

"Sign here," he said, "and be careful. It says 'fragile.'"

I looked at the return address: Baron, Kansas City, Missouri.

CHAPTER 41

Lucy

The cookies were chocolate crinkle and delicious, chewy at first but then melt-in-your-mouth. I ate two right there in the front hall and waited for flour power to take hold but, alas, no bags of money appeared.

O's letter was brief:

Dearest Beautiful Marvelous Lucy,

You know what your problem is?

It is not the money for camp like you think.

It is what Jenny would call a lack of GUMPTION!!!

You need to believe in yourself, and if you believe in yourself, you will get what you want.

Forgive me for going all Oprah on you. (LOL!)

But at the very least, if you believe in yourself, you will be less pathetic.

I admit I have never had a problem believing in myself. (It's getting other people to believe in me that's the problem.) But maybe because of that I see how being so modest all the time is hurting you—even from Kansas City, I see this.

So these cookies are to make you be brave and bold and stand up for yourself because you are just as important as anybody else and you deserve it.

Love always always always and FOREVER, O.

P.S. And see you at camp this summer FOR SURE! Your letter convinced me we all have to go and be back in Flowerpot Cabin again. I just talked to my mom about it, and she had her assistant make some calls. So now you have to come too. (Do I sound like Emma? LOL.)

O's letter did not cheer me up. I didn't need "gumption." I needed money—or maybe a normal family like other people have. In case you can't tell, I was in a pretty bad mood, so maybe it was good I had to leave my house and wrangle the triplets that afternoon.

Kendall's husband was away, and she was having a get-together for some girlfriends on the patio, starting at four thirty. I was going over at four o'clock. Arlo, Mia, Levi, and I would have a picnic on the lawn—well out of the way, as Kendall put it. Since O had sent a zillion cookies, I packed a paper bag with some to take with me.

"Bye, Mom! Bye, Nana!" I called as I left. If either one replied, I didn't hear.

On the short walk, I thought some more about O's note. Maybe if I had more "gumption," I would have said to myself, *"What does she know? She's crazy! I am self-confident and bold! I am!"* But because I don't have any gumption, I agreed with her. I did need more self-confidence.

But how were cookies supposed to help me get it?

And even if they did, how would self-confidence get me to Moonlight Ranch?

Kendall was waiting by the front door as usual, but the triplets were not.

"I couldn't take it anymore and violated one of my own rules," Kendall explained. "I let them watch TV after nap."

My brain heard her words, but I wasn't thinking about TV. So what I said was, "Kendall, do you think I have gumption?"

Kendall laughed. "Gumption! What an old-fashioned word!"

"It's one that Jenny uses," I said.

Kendall nodded. "And Jenny is . . . ?"

"Olivia's housekeeper," I said.

"Right!" said Kendall. "So I guess if I knew who Olivia was, I would understand perfectly."

"Yes," I said, "you would. Do I have it?"

"Uh . . ." Kendall seemed to be stalling. "Well, it isn't the first word that comes to mind when I think of you, Lucy. But maybe you do. Deep down. Come on, let's go get the triplets."

In the TV room, the triplets had made a tent out of blankets. Levi saw me first and scrambled up and out, pulling down blankets on his siblings. Mia and Arlo squealed in protest. Then they saw me and untangled themselves.

It was nice being even more interesting than SpongeBob.

"Lucy!"

"Woo-see!"

"Lucy!"

I gave them a group hug.

"We go play outside." Arlo tugged my arm.

"We have a jungle picnic," Levi said.

"We go play soccer," Mia said.

"Chips!" All three of them said at once. Then they looked at their mom, and she grinned sheepishly.

"I said they could have chips when you got here."

Aha—no wonder I was so interesting.

"What's in the paper bag?" Arlo asked me.

"Surprise," I said.

"Goody!" said Mia.

"Can we eat it?" asked Levi.

"You'll see," I said.

In the kitchen, Kendall had filled a cooler with picnic items. I picked it up and asked the triplets, "Who wants to carry the picnic blanket?"

"Not me!" "Not me!" "Not me!"

"Okay." I shrugged. "Then I'll carry it."

"No, *me!*" "No, *me!*" "No, *me!*"

I gave the blanket to Mia, who draped it over her shoulders like a cloak and then stuck her tongue out at her brothers.

"Lucky." Levi sulked.

"You take the soccer ball," I said.

"What about me?" Arlo asked.

I took the thermos out of the cooler and handed it to him. "You carry this. Now the cooler won't be so heavy."

"Tire them out," Kendall whispered. "Then read them a story. They've been watching TV so long, I bet they've got ants in their pants."

The triplets heard that last part, which they thought was hilarious. Before they could pull down one another's pants to check, I said, "Last one to the picnic spot is a rotten egg!"

Out the French doors and across the patio they tumbled—almost colliding with the early arrivals to their mom's get-together. The ladies all wore short summer dresses, shiny sandals, and coral-colored lipstick. They smiled and waved manicured hands and made a fuss over the triplets.

"Adorable," they said. "Darling." And, "How does she manage with three? I can barely handle one!"

The triplets stood up a little straighter, aware someone was paying attention to them. Then they forgot about it and sprinted for the far reaches of the yard. There, each of us took a corner of the tablecloth and pulled to spread it out. But for the sound of the women on the patio and cars in the distance, we felt very far away from civilization. It was easy to pretend we were off in a meadow in the wilderness.

Kendall had provided us with egg salad sandwiches with watercress, sugar snap peas, and *chips*—the highlight for the kids. They ate without fighting and kept glancing at the paper bag that held O's cookies. They didn't want to risk losing their surprise.

Is this an example of flour power? I wondered.

"Time for the surprise!" Arlo crowed.

"You're right," I said and—with a flourish—I opened the paper bag to reveal the chocolate crinkle cookies.

The *oohs* and *aahs* were immediately followed by, "Gimme! Gimme!" from Arlo, who reached for a cookie before they were even out of the bag.

Mia said, "Rude!"

"Am not!" said Arlo.

"He is rude, isn't he, Lucy?" Mia said.

"It's best not to grab cookies," I answered.

"I want a cookie *now*!" Arlo squealed.

Levi just smiled, glad he was not in trouble.

I was annoyed. This was what I got for sharing my

very special cookies with four-year-olds. I took a bit more time than necessary to remove the cookies from the bag and set them on a paper plate. The triplets looked on like dogs waiting for a treat. Then, all of a sudden, the obedience was just too much for Arlo, who stood up and announced, "I don't want any old stupid cookies!" and marched away.

"Oh dear," I said. "Arlo? Come back, sweetie. We want you to share cookies with us."

Mia and Levi, still on their best behavior, nodded solemnly.

But Arlo said, "No!" and kept walking.

He was headed toward the now shadowy fence line of the property, only a few yards away. He couldn't exactly escape. There was no place for him to go without running into a fence. Knowing the thought of cookies would bring him back eventually, I decided to let him sulk.

Mia, Levi, and I shared our cookies in happy silence. I was impressed that neither wolfed theirs and demanded a second. They seemed to understand that these cookies were special.

I was dreaming of milk when Mia, sitting across from me, turned her head and asked, "What dat?" She was looking in Arlo's direction.

Levi turned his head the same way and smiled. "Doggy!"

Doggy?

Now I looked too, and saw, weaving its way through the shrubbery, a shadow—muscular, powerful, and wild. This was not any kind of doggy I knew. For a few paralyzed moments I watched the shadow slink toward my four-year-old charge, my brain bubbling with unhelpful visions of sharp teeth.

I had to do something.

Arlo, meanwhile, was kneeling down looking at something on the ground, maybe an anthill. The first day I babysat, he was bitten by ants, and since then I had tried to get him to appreciate how interesting they are. Now he had no idea he was being stalked.

I was afraid to call out to him.

If he ran, the shadow would chase him—and the shadow would win.

I looked down for a rock to throw or a clump of

dirt—and saw a better weapon. Meanwhile, the gray shadow glided over the ground—closer and closer. It was now or never. I pivoted, shifted my weight, and swung my right leg—*thwack!* My instep connected squarely with the little green soccer ball, just the way Mrs. Kamae had taught us.

The sound made Arlo look up, and it startled Mia and Levi. The ball shot across the yard. The gray shadow dodged but too slowly. Hit in the flank, it lurched sideways, recovered, and ran off.

"Ha-ha-ha!" Levi pointed. "You hit the doggy with the ball!"

Mia shook her head, all disapproval. "Poor doggy! Mean, mean Lucy."

My heart pounded. I gulped air. Weak-kneed, I dropped to the grass in time to watch the coyote's tail disappear into the bushes. With the threat past, Arlo saw the coyote's tail retreating, realized what had almost happened, and screamed.

CHAPTER 42

Lucy

Mothers to the rescue! From the patio, they came running—wild-eyed and gripping the stems of their wineglasses.

For once my brain was keeping up with the world around me. I didn't want anyone to panic. I should act calm, say it was no big deal.

I did not get away with this, though, because Arlo shrieked, "Coyote!" the second his mom was in earshot.

Leave it to Arlo to recognize the animal—even though all he saw was its disappearing rear end. This is the danger of letting your child read too many nature books.

Safe in his mom's arms, Arlo began to cry, and then his siblings did too.

"Lucy?" Kendall looked at me.

I hesitated and Levi took over. "Woo-see kick soccer ball—*Pow! Boom!* It hit the doggy, and the doggy ran away!"

Mia nodded to confirm the story.

"All we really saw was a shadow near Arlo," I said as calmly as I could. "I'm not sure what it was. I kicked the ball to scare it away."

"Pow! Boom!" Levi repeated.

"Mean Lucy," Mia said.

"It was a *coyote*," Arlo repeated.

"Oh my goodness," murmured one of the other mothers, and Courtney's mother said, "A wild animal?"

"The triplets were in their own yard!"

"All those missing cats . . ."

"What if Lucy hadn't been there?"

"What if Lucy hadn't thought so quickly?"

"What if Lucy didn't have such good aim?"

Kendall pulled Arlo a little closer and looked me in the eye. "You're a hero," she said.

"How were Arnold, Leland, and Matilda tonight?" Nana asked when I got home.

For once I set her straight. "*Arlo*, *Levi*, and *Mia* are fine."

Nana didn't appear to notice my correction. "And how was their mom's party?"

"I guess the ladies had fun," I said. "There was, uh, some excitement with an animal in the yard, but I chased it away."

"An animal?"

"Arlo thought it was a coyote. It looked like one," I said. I kind of wanted to tell her the story. It was the most excitement I'd had in a while—maybe ever.

But Nana said, "It was probably somebody's dog."

So then I wasn't so eager to talk about it. "Yeah, maybe."

If Mom came in later after her shift, I didn't wake up.

* * *

The next day—Sunday—something felt different. I don't mean I felt like I was a hero or anything. But not just anyone has a knack with a soccer ball. Maybe it *was* lucky for Arlo that I was the one who was there.

Then I thought some more about "gumption." I did want Mom and Nana to know I'd done something good. Mom would be all about celebrating with me. Maybe Nana would, too. You could never tell.

So I went to my mom's bedroom, and then I went to Nana's, and in both places I announced we were having tea and cookies in the living room at ten.

"Tea and cookies at ten in the morning?" Nana said. "I have never heard of such a thing."

"Be there," I said, "or be square."

"Are you sure everything is all right?" Nana narrowed her eyes at me. "Why are we convening in the living room of all places?"

"Because we have a living room," I said, "so we should use it. Anyway, I got some cookies in the mail from Olivia—Olivia from camp. And I want to share."

Reluctant as they were, my mother and grand-mother both showed up at ten. They sat themselves at opposite ends of the rarely used sofa. I poured the tea—chamomile, because it is supposed to be calming.

The plate of cookies lay on the coffee table. "What kind of cookies are they?" Nana asked.

"Good cookies. Here." I held the plate out to her.

Nana didn't move. "They *look* all right," she said.

"Oh, for cripe's sake, Mother, have a cookie," said my mom. "They're not bacteria specimens. Just eat one."

Nana frowned at my mother, looked back at the plate, and finally selected a cookie. My mom reached over and took two.

We sipped our tea and ate. After a minute, Nana looked at my mother. "Why don't you ever paint any-more?" she asked.

"What?" my mom said. "Where did that question come from? And anyway, when would I paint? If you haven't noticed, I have a job now."

"You only work the dinner shift," said my grandmother.

"Beyond that, if you weren't so busy gallivanting around the countryside with this flame or that, you would have time to paint."

"It's none of your business if I paint," my mother said. "And I don't have a 'flame' at the moment—so leave me alone."

"You're a good artist when you want to be," my grandmother said. "And you're always saying I tear you down. So here I try to be encouraging, and see where it gets me."

"Change of topic," I announced. "How do you like the cookies?"

This made my grandmother smile—a rare show of enthusiasm. "They are exquisite! Is Olivia the one who's a barbecue sauce heiress?"

"She hates it when people say that," my mother put in.

"I didn't say it in front of her," Nana said.

"Let's open the drapes," I said.

"Better not," said Mom, "unless you want to see all the dirt."

I ignored her, got up, and pulled the cord so that all

of a sudden the drapes were wide open. The sunlight revealed the streaked windows, the shabbiness, the cat shreds, and the dust—but even so, it was more cheerful than sitting in the dark.

"I have a story to tell you," I said, "about something that happened yesterday."

CHAPTER 43

May 25

Dear Lucy,

I saw you on the TV news. Until then, I never knew you were (1) brave in the face of wild predators and (2) good at soccer.

Congratulations!

Besides writing what I just wrote, I have three

more reasons for writing. (1) Are you going to Moonlight Ranch again this summer? (2) Do you happen to know if Grace Xi is going? (3) Do you know anything about the four boxes of cookies that have come to my house in the mail this year?

None of the boxes had notes or return addresses. But I noticed the postmarks were California, Massachusetts, Pennsylvania, and Missouri. These are the home states of you, Grace, Emma, and Olivia—all the girls in Flowerpot Cabin. I checked the camp directory.

The cookies were all different kinds, but they were all very good. Luckily, I like nuts and chocolate.

Write back, please.
Yours very sincerely,
Vivek Sonti

P.S. I am going to Moonlight Ranch this summer because my parents will be in India. If you go too, perhaps we will see each other. It is not such a very big place.

CHAPTER 44

May 30

Dear Vivek,

Thank you for your letter.
I did not really deserve so much
attention for saving Arlo's life. Lots
of people are good at kicking soccer
balls, and I was super surprised when
the TV people called and then there

were all those cameras. It was kind of
embarrassing.

Then later something else happened
that wasn't on TV. Animal control police
came to my neighborhood and shot the
coyote with a dart that made it go to
sleep. My mom told me that after that
they took it to the forest far away and
set it free so it could have a happy life.

My nana told me that's a crock of
hooey, and the coyote is now in coyote
heaven. Nana says that's a good thing,
too, because otherwise it would have come
back again.

I don't know who to believe. But I know
who I want to believe.

About Moonlight Ranch, I have to
tell you a story. After the thing with
the coyote, I asked my mom and my
grandmother if they would please pay to
send me to camp this summer.

Nana said no.

Then my mom gave her a look (if you have a mom, you might know this look) and Nana said maybe.

Then my mom asked, "What about Lucy's babysitting money? You have been saving it for her."

Nana said the babysitting money wasn't enough. My mom asked how much not enough?

But guess what! It turned out that after almost a year of babysitting, my savings almost WERE enough! And now that my mom is working, she can help pay the difference.

So the answer is yes. I will be at Moonlight Ranch this summer.

While I am telling stories, here is one about cookies. I was making a bricolage (look it up) for art class, and it didn't quite seem finished. Then Olivia happened to send me a box of cookies, and I realized what I needed to finish it was a single, solitary cookie. So I sacrificed eating one and sprayed it with clear plastic and attached it with thread to my project, and my art teacher entered it in the citywide elementary art show, and it won a blue ribbon!!!

Sorry this was such a long letter. I hope we see each other at camp.

Sincerely,
Lucy Ambrose

P.S. What a strange coincidence about all the cookies you got in the mail this year!

CHAPTER 45

Tuesday, May 31

Hannah hadn't planned to work at Moonlight Ranch that summer. She had already sent back the form that said no. She was going to take an internship closer to home, in Manhattan.

Then, on the Tuesday after Memorial Day, Buck, the camp director, phoned. "Please come back this summer. We've had a rather unusual request, and we'd like to honor it if we can."

"What request?" Hannah asked. She was sitting on the edge of her bed at home in Floral Park, New York—a town on Long Island. She was supposed to meet her boyfriend at Starbucks, and she was late.

"I'd rather not name names," the camp director said. "The short of it is that we'd like you to be counselor in Flowerpot Cabin with the same campers as last summer."

"The same campers? Grace, Emma, Olivia, and Lucy?"

"Yes."

Hannah hesitated. She had been picturing a job at a museum, wearing nice clothes and high heels, taking the subway to work, meeting friends for dinner.

It required a radical brain shift to picture instead clear blue sky, hot desert air, the horse barn—and four girls with strong personalities, managing them and keeping them happy.

In the instant before answering, Hannah pictured each of their faces smiling (even Grace!). She wondered if they had used her grandfather's recipes.

Hannah hesitated longer than she meant to,

but—isn't life funny?—this turned out to be good. Buck said, "All right, we'll offer a raise in pay. We really do want you to come back."

"Totally!" Hannah said impulsively. "I will totally come back this summer."

Hannah heard Buck's sigh from two thousand miles away. "Oh, good. We can't wait to see you and your campers back at Moonlight Ranch."

CHAPTER 46

Wednesday, June 1

Dear Vivek,

Lucy telephoned and said you wrote her a letter after she was on TV for saving Arlo from being eaten by the coyote.

This reminded me that I owe you a thank-you note.

If my parents knew it had taken me ten

months to write a thank-you note they
would be very disappointed.

Thank you very much for the packet of
Oreo cookies. Coincidentally, they are my
favorite. Even though you only gave them to
me because you bought them by mistake, it
was still very kind.

Here is something funny. I haven't opened
the packet yet. They are in a drawer in my
desk. I am pretty sure Oreo cookies never go
bad. Sugar is a natural preservative.

Lucy said you will be at Moonlight Ranch
this summer. I will be there too.

Sincerely,
Grace Xi

Hey, cookie bakers!

Baking is a blast, but make sure you ask an adult for help with the oven or mixer. Have fun!

XX, Hannah

Grandpa's Chocolate Chip Cookies

Anybody can make chocolate chip cookies, but these have a couple of Grandpa's secrets to make them light and chewy.

(Makes about 4 dozen)

1 cup (2 sticks) softened unsalted butter

1 cup white sugar

1 cup packed brown sugar

2 eggs

2 teaspoons vanilla extract

1 teaspoon baking soda

2 teaspoons hot water

½ teaspoon salt

2 cups all-purpose flour

1 cup oat flour (see note)

2 cups semisweet chocolate chips (preferably Ghirardelli)

1 cup chopped pecans (optional)

Preheat oven to 350°F. In the large bowl of a mixer, cream together butter and both sugars until smooth. Beat in the eggs one at a time, then stir in the vanilla. Dissolve the baking soda in hot water and add to batter along with salt. Stir in flour, oat flour, chocolate chips, and pecans (if using). Drop by tablespoonfuls onto ungreased cookie sheets. Bake for about 10 minutes or until the edges are just brown.

Note: For oat flour, grind a scant 1 ¼ cups old-fashioned rolled oats (not instant and not steel cut) in a food processor for about five seconds to yield 1 cup oat flour.

Grandpa's Iced Holiday Cookies

These have a satisfying texture and are more flavorful than iced cookies from a bakery. Also, the dough is easy to work with. Be sure to allow time to chill the dough and let cookies cool before icing.

(Makes about 5 dozen)

3 cups all-purpose flour

1 teaspoon baking powder

½ teaspoon salt

1 cup (2 sticks) unsalted butter, at room temperature

1 cup sugar

1 large egg

2 tablespoons sour cream

1 teaspoon vanilla extract

Additional sugar for rolling out cookies

For the cookies, sift the flour, baking powder, and salt into a medium bowl. Then, in the large bowl of an electric mixer, beat the butter and one cup sugar until well blended. Add the egg, sour cream, and vanilla, and beat

1 minute. In two additions, add the sifted dry ingredients and beat until just blended.

Divide the dough in half and flatten each half into a disk. Wrap the disks in plastic and chill at least 1 hour and up to 1 day. If dough is refrigerated more than an hour, let it sit out a few minutes to soften before you roll it out.

Sprinkle a work surface and the top of the dough disks with additional sugar. Working one disk at a time, roll the dough to ¼-inch thickness and cut out with assorted 2- to 3-inch cookie cutters. Transfer to cookie sheets lined with parchment paper, spacing 1 inch apart. Keep gathering scraps, rolling dough and cutting cookies until all the dough is used. Chill unbaked cookies on baking sheets at least 15 minutes and up to 1 hour before baking.

Preheat oven to 350°F. Bake cookies, one sheet at a time, until golden at the edges, about 12 minutes. Transfer cookies to racks and cool completely before icing.

Icing

4 cups sifted powdered sugar

3 tablespoons milk

½ teaspoon vanilla extract

Colored sugar crystals, sprinkles, and/or decorations

Food-safe colored markers

For the icing, stir together powdered sugar, milk, and vanilla until smooth and spreadable. Add more milk by the teaspoonful if the mixture is too thick, and sugar if it is too thin.

With an icing spatula or table knife, spread a thin layer of icing on each cookie. Sprinkle on sugar crystals and other decorations before icing sets. Let icing dry about half an hour before using markers.

Cookies can be made up to 3 days ahead. Store air-tight between sheets of waxed paper at room temperature.

Grandpa's Big Chocolate Cookies

These are easy to make in a saucepan (!) and taste like brownies in cookie disguise.

(Makes about 2 dozen)

2 teaspoons instant coffee

¼ cup boiling water

2 ounces (2 squares) unsweetened baker's chocolate, chopped

6 tablespoons (¾ stick) softened unsalted butter

½ teaspoon vanilla extract

1 cup sugar

2 eggs

1 cup sifted all-purpose flour

¼ teaspoon salt

2 cups chopped walnuts (optional)

1 cup chocolate chips (preferably Ghirardelli)

Preheat oven to 350°F. In a saucepan, dissolve coffee in hot water. Add chocolate and place over low heat to melt the chocolate, stirring constantly.

In the large bowl of an electric mixer, beat the butter, then add vanilla and sugar till combined. Add the cooled chocolate mixture (it's okay if it's still warm but it should not be hot) and beat until smooth. Add the eggs one at a time, beating until blended.

Combine flour and salt, and add to saucepan. Stir in nuts and chocolate chips.

Place dough by the teaspoonful on a parchment-lined cookie sheet about 2 inches apart. Bake about 13 minutes. Cookies are done if the center barely springs back when touched. Do not overbake. Cool on a rack immediately.

Grandpa's Chocolate Crinkle Cookies

These melt in your mouth like cotton candy, and the powdered sugar makes a pretty pattern on top. Be sure to allow time for chilling!

(Makes about 6 dozen)

½ cup vegetable oil

4 ounces (4 squares) unsweetened baker's chocolate, melted and cooled

2 cups sugar

2 teaspoons vanilla extract

4 eggs

2 cups all-purpose flour

2 teaspoons baking powder

½ teaspoon salt

nonstick cooking spray

½ cup powdered sugar

In a large bowl, mix the oil, chocolate, sugar, and vanilla. Stir in the eggs, one at a time. Stir in the flour, baking powder, and salt. Cover and refrigerate at least 3 hours.

Heat the oven to 350°F. Grease a cookie sheet with non-stick cooking spray.

Drop the dough by teaspoonfuls into powdered sugar. Roll to coat and shape into balls. Place cookies about 2 inches apart on cookie sheets. Bake 10 to 12 minutes. To test for doneness, touch gently in the center with a teaspoon. Almost no imprint should remain. Remove to cooling racks immediately.

If you liked

THE SECRET COOKIE CLUB,

read more adventures of the girls of Flowerpot Cabin in

CAMPFIRE COOKIES.

Read on for a sneak peek and activities!

The scorpions, tarantulas, and rattlesnakes that live just outside the Moonlight Ranch main gate stay well out of the way on Camper Arrival Day, when the bare patch of ground they call home is overrun with human activity—cars pulling in and out, meetings and reunions, parents helping campers with heavy loads of luggage.

Scorpions, tarantulas, and rattlesnakes are shy and

peace-loving creatures. They want nothing to do with so much action.

While a few Moonlight Ranch campers always arrive on their own by shuttle from the Phoenix airport, most drive in with their parents. That late-June morning, families began arriving at ten, and by ten forty-five, Hannah Lehrer from Long Island, New York, was having second thoughts about her decision to come back for a second summer as counselor in Flowerpot Cabin.

Beside her stood the reason for those second thoughts, Olivia Baron, a tall, striking eleven-year-old black girl with drama queen tendencies and a scary-good vocabulary.

Hannah knew Olivia well. Hannah had been her counselor the year before and had greeted Olivia with a big hug when she alighted from the Cadillac SUV her parents had rented for the drive. After that, the two had chatted eagerly about the summer to come.

"This year Flowerpot Cabin will totally dominate Chore Score!" Olivia announced. "Purple Sage is going down!"

Purple Sage was another ten-to-eleven girls cabin, and Chore Score, the daily measure of how thoroughly cabins were cleaned, was a big deal at Moonlight Ranch.

Hannah laughed. "My friend Jane's the counselor in Purple Sage again this year."

"What about the campers?" Olivia asked.

"One returning, the others new," said Hannah.

"I hope it's not that Brianna girl coming back," said Olivia. "She is *stuck-up!*"

"Come on, O. She's not that bad," said Hannah. "O" was Olivia's nickname.

"Oh, no-o-o!" Olivia moaned. "That means she *is* the one coming back! Is she here yet?"

"I don't think so," Hannah said. "Jane told me she's coming on one of the airport shuttles. Can I help you, Mrs. Baron? That crate looks heavy."

"It is! And thank you, Hannah." Together they hefted the crate up and onto a handcart already piled with Olivia's possessions. "What have you got in here, anyway, Livia?" her mom asked.

"That one?" Olivia studied it for a moment. "My backup iPad, my speakers, some batteries, some chargers, a game platform, controller, video monitor . . . and I think extra shoes."

Hannah's heart sank. "Uh, Olivia? Mrs. Baron? You know about the new no-electronics policy, right? You signed the contract. You must've."

"What's that mean—no electronics?" Olivia asked.

"Oh, dear," said Mrs. Baron. "My assistant sent in the paperwork. What is it that I missed?"

Anticipating that some parents might need a refresher on the policy, the camp director had given each counselor a copy of the letter describing it. Now Hannah pulled out the letter, unfolded it, and handed it to Olivia's mom.

Dear Moonlight Ranch families,

More than half a century ago, my parents established a sleepaway camp at their beautiful working cattle ranch in central Arizona. At first the camp was a modest affair, but over time it has grown into the nationally renowned operation that you know so well.

My own Moonlight Ranch journey began when I was a boy barely old enough to flake hay. I have seen many changes in the ensuing years, one of which brings me to my point in writing to you today. Recently, our highly qualified and caring professional staff has observed that our campers, like young people the world over, engage ever more frequently with their electronic devices.

The result, in too many cases, is that campers physically surrounded by our beautiful and expansive environment are mentally buried in the same restrictive screen experience they could have in their bedrooms at home.

For this reason, we at Moonlight Ranch have decided to declare camp property an electronics-free zone for the upcoming summer. No electronic devices of any kind, including cellular telephones, will be permitted. If parents need to get in touch with their campers, they may call Paula in the camp office anytime, day or night. Likewise, campers urgently needing to contact parents will have access to Paula around the clock.

In addition, all campers will be expected to write at least one letter home per week. In the same spirit, parents may wish to reciprocate by writing cards and letters to their campers.

To minimize misunderstanding and ensure that summer gets off to a smooth start, a contract outlining the no-electronics agreement is enclosed for your signature.

Thank you for your understanding, and we look forward to another rewarding summer for your sons and daughters here with our livestock in the wholesome Arizona desert.

Sincerely,

Jonathan S. "Buck" Cooper, Camp Director

P.S. As always, if you have any questions, please contact Paula in the camp office.

Olivia read over her mom's shoulder. As she did, her hand sought out the phone in the pocket of her shorts. By the time Mrs. Baron was done reading, Olivia was gripping her phone with white-knuckled devotion.

"I can't live without it!" she cried. "My friends will forget I exist!"

"Oh, darling. I am sorry," Mrs. Baron said. "I should have read this before. But don't you think it might be a nice idea to go a short while without all your gizmos? I wish I could give that a try."

This comment did not help matters. In fact, it catapulted Olivia into full-on drama queen mode. "A whole summer is *not* a *short while*!" she wailed. "You don't understand *anything*!"

It was then that Hannah questioned her decision to return to Moonlight Ranch.

To keep from saying something she'd regret, Hannah turned and looked across the desert. In her mind's eye, she saw the marble-lined corridors of the New York museum where she could have worked that summer, the dresses and high heels she'd be wearing, the weekends at the beach with her friends.

And she saw the best part of this parallel summer, her new boyfriend, Travis. He was the first real boyfriend she had ever had.

What am I doing out here in the middle of nowhere? she thought. *The sunshine is too bright. The air smells like dust and horses. My new jeans scratch, and my boots are heavy. My face feels sticky with sweat and sunscreen.*

To top it off, I'm arguing with an eleven-year-old!

Hannah sighed and mentally shook herself. This was the summer she had chosen. It was time to step up.

"Olivia?" She looked back at her camper. "During camp, your social life is here, and no one else has a phone either. Sorry, but you're going to have to leave that crate behind. And hand over your phone, too."

Slam! Olivia's dad closed the hatch of the SUV and turned to Hannah, smiling. "Whoa," he said, then, "Livia"—he looked at his daughter—"I think you might have met your match."

Olivia's dad was George Baron of Baron Barbecue Sauce, a staple on the shelves of every grocery store in

America. His and his wife's faces were even on the label. On the scale of Moonlight Ranch celebrities, the two of them were right up there with Brianna's mom, Natalya Silverbug, a former model who now sold a high-tech brand of dust mop on a shopping network.

Olivia folded her arms across her chest and set her jaw. She looked ready to do battle for her right to keep her phone. Then, all of a sudden, she backed down. "Oh, all right, fine." She pulled the phone from her pocket and handed it to her mom. "I guess I can live without it for one summer. It'll be good for me, right?"

Hannah wondered what had caused Olivia to change her mind so abruptly—but she was too grateful to say anything.

Mrs. Baron looked surprised too, but then recovered. "Exactly," she said, "and writing letters is fun. I'll send you some stickers to make them pretty, and some markers if you want. How would that be?"

"That would be cool, Mama," said Olivia. "Thank you."

Olivia's father shot Hannah a look that said thumbs-up. At the same time, a voice came from across the parking area. "Hannah! Over here!"

THE SECRET COOKIE CLUB'S

BIG BATCH of BFF ACTIVITIES

Paula Wiseman Books · Simon & Schuster Children's Publishing

THE
YUMMY COOKIE
PERSONALITY QUIZ

What type of cookie matches your personality? Answer the questions below to find out!

1. What's your favorite thing to do with friends?

A. Something simple, like going to see a movie or hanging out in a coffee shop.

B. You're happy just to spend a day in, chatting with close friends.

C. If you can't throw a party, you want to find one: rock climbing, mountain biking, or camping!

D. Get together to play games—the more challenging, the better!

2. What do you do for fun when you're on your own?

A. Cook or bake something to share next time you're with friends.

B. Draw, play music, or do something crafty.

C. Head out to the park or a movie on your own.

D. Read, journal, or just spend time with your thoughts.

3. When you're sitting in class and the teacher asks a tough question, what do you do?

A. If you know the answer, you'll definitely raise your hand and see if the teacher calls on you.

B. You keep your hand down, even though you know the right answer—you're too shy to speak in front of the whole class!

C. Raise your hand right away! You're not sure if you know the answer but you'll give it a shot.

D. You're shouting the right answer out even before your hand's all the way in the air!

4. A little style question: how do you like to wear your hair?

A. A classic ponytail—cute, but out of your face.

B. You tie it up in a neat bun.

C. You let it do its own thing, whether that's wavy, curly, or straight.

D. You keep it short and stylish, like a pixie cut.

ANSWER KEY

MOSTLY A'S:

CHOCOLATE CHIP!

You're classic and reliable, the kind of person who's loved by all. You're always there for a friend in need, and you help others see the joy in simple pleasures. But you may sometimes forget to take care of the most important person in your life: YOU!

MOSTLY B'S:

SNICKERDOODLE!

Those who don't know you well see you as classy and predictable—which may be true—but your close friends know you're full of little surprises. You're genuinely sweet, but it takes a little pushing to get you out of your shell.

MOSTLY C'S:

PEANUT BUTTER!

You're always up for a party, a new experience, or a practical joke. You inspire strong feelings in those around you—not everyone can keep up with you, but those who can know that you're a friend for life.

MOSTLY D'S:

GINGERSNAP!

You're one smart cookie! You might have been raised as a bit of a hippy, but you're more hip than anything else, and you always say exactly what's on your mind—even if you sometimes have trouble taking your own advice.

NEW BFFS!

Who are your best friends? Keep a record of one of them here—
or make copies and keep a record of all of them!

NEW BFFS

MY NAME:

MY AGE:

MY BEST FRIEND'S NAME:

MY BEST FRIEND'S AGE:

I LIKE MY FRIEND BECAUSE...

_____

_____

_____

_____

_____

_____

WORD SEARCH

What are your favorite things to do with friends?
See if you can find all of these great BFF activities in the word search below

BAKE	EMAIL	PRETEND	DOGWALK
DRAW	MUSIC	GAMES	SPORTS
HIKE	LEARN	READ	PHONE

```
D  W  N  Y  C  W  W  F
P  O  S  P  O  R  T  S
H  R  G  C  O  X  Q  H
O  E  L  W  I  H  H  I
N  A  F  I  A  S  Q  K
E  D  X  V  A  L  U  E
L  E  A  R  N  M  K  M
G  A  M  E  S  R  E  L
K  P  R  E  T  E  N  D
B  A  K  E  D  R  A  W
```

LETTER WRITING CHALLENGE

Are you ready to be a real member of the club?
Complete all the activities below, then copy and cut out your membership card!

1. Write and send a letter to your BFF!

2. Email your favorite cookie recipe to at least three friends, and ask them to write back with their own.

3. Start a cookie club of your own! Decide who will bake for whom, and when. Then get started! Don't forget to write, call, or email each other to keep up on each other's lives, so you know who needs cookies most, and for what.

• OFFICIAL MEMBER OF •

THE

SECRET COOKIE CLUB

(YOUR NAME HERE!)